Disney

Tim Burton's The Nightmare Before Christmas

Disney

Tim Burton's The Nightmare Before Christmas

ADAPTED BY *NEW YORK TIMES* BEST-SELLING AUTHOR

Megan Shepherd

SCHOLASTIC
SYDNEY AUCKLAND NEW YORK TORONTO LONDON MEXICO CITY
NEW DELHI HONG KONG BUENOS AIRES PUERTO RICO

Published by Scholastic Australia in 2024.

Scholastic Australia Pty Limited
PO Box 579 Gosford NSW 2250
ABN 11 000 614 577
www.scholastic.com.au

Part of the Scholastic Group
Sydney • Auckland • New York • Toronto • London • Mexico City • New Delhi
Hong Kong • Buenos Aires • Puerto Rico

ISBN 978-1-76152-600-8

Printed in China.

Scholastic Australia's policy, in association with its printers, is to use papers that are renewable and made efficiently from wood grown in responsibly managed forests, so as to minimise its environmental footprint.

"I'M
AFRAID
I'VE MADE
A TERRIBLE MESS
OF YOUR HOLIDAY."

—Jack Skellington

Disney

Tim Burton's The Nightmare Before Christmas

PROLOGUE

THE HINTERLANDS

AT THE EDGE of the living world, the Hinterlands began. In this land between land, no leaves sprouted from the trees' branches. No birdsong coasted on the wind. Light always entered at a slant, as though it was perpetual dawn or dusk, when shadows were at their longest.

Few travelers had ever set foot in the Hinterlands, and those who did returned with curious tales about curious things, like a November breeze that greeted them at the entrance to the forest, tickling the hair on their arms like the breath of a ghost. The trees there were not quite pine and not quite oak but rather something in between. When one wanderer pressed a calloused palm to the bark, he swore he felt an odd warmth: the spirit of the Hinterlands.

Most travelers turned back, suspicious of the forest, but the few who pressed on climbed a rise and stumbled upon a ring of seven trees tall enough to scrape the clouds with the fingerlike tips of their branches. When the wind urged them closer, the wanderers discovered carved images in the bark; each trunk bore a symbol from the holiday worlds of old:

an unlit firework decorated with white stars,
a scarlet-red heart,
a four-leaf clover,
an egg painted with yellows and pinks and blues,
a stout turkey,
an evergreen tree decorated with tinsel and tiny
gingerbread men,
a pumpkin carved into a grinning ghoulish face.

While exploring the circle of trees, some travelers felt a fresh breeze ruffle their hair. Others saw the sizzle of spent fireworks. A few heard the tinkling of sleigh bells or the laughter of children. More than one wanderer smelled the mouth-watering aroma of pumpkin pie.

Only the wind—and whoever had etched the shapes into the trees many, many years earlier—knew the truth about the carvings: they were much more than symbols.

They were *doors.*

When a few brave souls twisted the hidden doorknobs with trembling hands, they found dark tunnels on the other side. One ended in a snowy wonderland. The next opened to clover fields. Another led to a sky bursting with fireworks, and another to a garden where fat little cherubs flew around, wielding heart-shaped arrows.

A voice that was somehow both familiar and new reverberated among the trees:

"'Twas a long time ago, longer now than it seems,
in a place that perhaps you've seen in your dreams.
For the story that you are about to be told
took place in the holiday worlds of old.
Now, you've probably wondered where holidays
come from.
If you haven't, I'd say it's time you begun . . ."

Only the bravest wanderers dared to approach the most gnarled tree in the clearing. The wind carried the echo of a hundred screams as those bold few reached for the doorknob nose of the devilishly grinning jack-o'-lantern and opened the doorway to a land of dreams—or, as they soon discovered, *nightmares.*

CHAPTER ONE

0 DAYS TILL HALLOWEEN

W*HAT A NIGHT!*

The moon was full and fat as a procession of monsters returned from the land of the living back to their home of Halloween Town. Dead leaves skittered around their heels as they followed a sign held by a pumpkin-headed scarecrow that directed them to the town's gate. The town itself rose high on a hill, full of angular buildings with tangerine lights glowing in the windows and creaky iron fences festooned with jack-o'-lanterns. Overhead a sinister shadow eclipsed the moon, only to burst into a cluster of bats. As they neared the gate, every resident, from the hulking Behemoth to the tiniest flea, agreed that it had been the most shriek-filled, terror-inducing Halloween anyone could remember.

Their voices rang out as they celebrated their most beloved night: "This is Halloween!"

Their haunting words painted a terrifying picture of a night filled with mayhem and mischief. The Creature Under the Bed cackled as he recalled lying in wait beneath a checkered bedspread, with his sharp teeth and glowing red eyes. The Creature Under the Stairs wiggled his snakelike fingers, which had hissed at boys and girls. The Harlequin Demon jumped out of a trash can at the same time the Wolfman burst through a stone wall, followed by the Melting Man popping up from the sewer. The Clown with the Tear-Away Face tottered back and forth on his unicycle, ripping away his face to reveal nothing but a hollow void. And soaring above them all, a pair of witch sisters snickered as they raced on their brooms, recounting tales of the night's exploits to the jack-o'-lantern heads in the pumpkin patch below.

The two-faced mayor of Halloween Town marshaled the procession with an extra spring in his step. His top hat was narrow and so elongated that it nearly doubled his height. He wore the favorite of his two faces, a rosy-cheeked one with a maniacal grin. Like any good elected official, he knew how to make a dramatic entrance.

On the other side of the gates, the Town Square was empty except for a few spiders and rats and the handful of monstrous youngsters who weren't old enough for their first Halloween scares. The Winged Demon and the Corpse Kid gasped when they heard the jubilant crowd returning. They abandoned the torture game they'd been playing, letting the guillotine slam down on a pumpkin and split it cleanly in two, and rushed toward the gates just steps behind the Corpse Kid's undead parents. Meanwhile, perched high over town inside a nearby castle, a rag doll gripped the bars of her cell window, listening to the procession as she combed her long red hair with a broken jawbone.

The creaky iron gate rattled itself to life at the gatekeeper's command and rose to allow the procession to enter. Mr. Hyde and the Devil were the first through the gates, followed by the Mayor, who rode proudly atop the official town hearse. He threw open his arms in triumph, even though the only person he'd managed to scare all night had been a sneezy little boy with hay fever.

Lights flickered in the windows of the houses, like grinning jack-o'-lanterns. The night was velvet-black and starless, lit only by the moon and the greenish glow of the fountain bubbling slime in the center of the Town Square. Creatures of all shapes and states of decay paraded in a spiraling pattern around the fountain. Despite the ax permanently embedded in the back of his skull, Behemoth hoisted a rope over his blue-fleshed shoulder, pulling a straw horse on wheels that carried the pumpkin-headed scarecrow from the fields outside town.

To everyone's surprise, the scarecrow atop the straw horse suddenly sprang to life. The crowd gasped. What clever devilry was this?

With spindly limbs that hinged like those of a daddy longlegs, the scarecrow crouched atop his steed, then jumped into the air with a flourish and threw himself into a pinwheel followed by a staggering pirouette.

The dancing scarecrow continued his astounding performance as his twiggy arm grabbed a torch from the crowd. Everyone fell into a hush. *Fire!* They marveled that a creature made of straw would dare to hold a torch. But instead of shying away from the flame, the scarecrow toyed with it as its orange tongue flicked higher. He even thrust the torch straight into his own pumpkin mouth, causing his straw body to catch fire.

The crowd gasped. Even the rag doll, who had snuck out of the castle she called home to join the festivities, peeked around the side of the Hanging Tree to gaze at the performance. Flames soon engulfed the scarecrow from fingertip to fingertip. His pumpkin skull started to roast. But the scarecrow continued to dance as flames ate away at his rumpled clothes and dry straw stuffing. He twirled and bowed. *A living, breathing, dancing bonfire!*

The crowd swayed with their claws and tentacles in the air as the scarecrow continued his feverish danse macabre. The monsters clapped in delight as he spun atop the straw horse, shooting off sparks. They leaned in greedily, anxious to watch the carnage.

Just when it seemed the flames would reduce him to ash, the scarecrow sprang nimbly from the back of the straw horse and dove headfirst into the fountain. Bluish smoke rose as the slime extinguished the flames. All traces of the dancing scarecrow disappeared beneath the surface.

The Corpse Kid and Mummy Boy leaned over the fountain to search for any signs of the scarecrow.

Towering over the rest of the crowd, the Hanging Tree stretched out its branches and shambled closer to let its dangling hanged men have a look. Swinging by their nooses, they peered into the slime, but even from their high vantage point, they could detect no trace of him.

Suddenly, the crowd hushed again. Rising straight out of the fountain's slime was . . . the scarecrow! Only now the scarecrow costume and pumpkin head were burned away, and a grinning skull rose proudly atop a skeletal body dressed in an elegant pinstripe suit, complete with a wide bat bow tie.

The mysterious scarecrow was the town's very own Pumpkin King, Jack Skellington!

CHAPTER TWO

0 DAYS TILL HALLOWEEN

APPLAUSE ERUPTED from the crowd at the appearance of their beloved Halloween leader.

The night's success was due to Jack Skellington, as it was every year. A debonair skeleton, Jack had once more delivered the most scares in a single night. His ghoulish grin had caused an entire sleepover party to burst into tears. His bone-clacking jig had made countless parents drop their trick-or-treaters' candy bags and run. Truly, the Pumpkin King had earned his title for another year—and his clever performance as the scarecrow had been the whipped cream on the pumpkin pie.

The witch sisters oohed and aahed at the handsome skeleton, tossing their pointed hats into the air as the rest of the townsfolk congratulated themselves on a job well done.

The Clown with the Tear-Away Face balanced on his tiny unicycle as he pinwheeled his arms in the air and exclaimed, "It's over!"

"We did it!" agreed Behemoth, offering his massive belly for a squishy chest bump with the clown.

"Wasn't it terrifying?" said the Wolfman, baring his claws at Mr. Hyde and the Cyclops in fond remembrance of the night's scares.

"What a night!" the two of them agreed. In his excitement, Mr. Hyde wrapped a chain around the Cyclops' neck, choking him, but the one-eyed monster's gagging soon turned into a giggle.

Still wearing his rosy face, the Mayor bounced

through the crowd, eager to be seen standing near Halloween Town's greatest star.

"Great Halloween, everybody!" he declared.

Jack continued to bow and wave away the praise of his adoring crowd, then nimbly stepped off the fountain as the monsters moved aside to make room for him.

"I believe it was our most horrible yet," Jack agreed with a gentlemanly bow from his great height. He pressed a bony hand to his rib cage. "Thank you, everyone."

"No, thanks to you, Jack," the Mayor chimed in. "Without your brilliant leadership—"

Jack waved away the praise. "Not at all, Mayor."

A vampire with gleaming fangs pressed in. "You're such a scream, Jack."

The witch sister with mossy curls elbowed her way to the front of the crowd, where she cooed, "You're a witch's fondest dream."

Not to be outdone, her green-skinned sister purred, "You made walls fall, Jack."

"Walls fall?" The first witch interrupted. "You made the very *mountains* crack, Jack!" She batted her cobweb-crusted eyelashes at him and flashed a smile that showed off the mold growing on her teeth.

Watching from behind the Hanging Tree, the rag doll, named Sally, giggled to herself at the sight of Jack fending off his many admirers. The thick stitching holding on her neck and arms was amateurish compared to the finer stitches that formed her dress of scrap fabrics—but that was to be expected: she'd sewn the dress herself, whereas her scientific-minded creator, Dr. Finkelstein, had inexpertly sewn *her*.

Dr. Finkelstein hadn't given Sally a heart—like her head, her chest was packed with dried leaves and rags—yet she somehow felt a phantom patter at the sight of the Pumpkin King. How happy she was to be here with the townsfolk instead of locked away in Dr. Finkelstein's castle. Thank goodness the deadly nightshade she had placed into her creator's tea had knocked him out long enough for her to escape.

Out of nowhere, a small black-gloved hand reached out and grabbed her wrist.

Sally gasped, trying to pull away.

Dr. Finkelstein leered up at her through the dark glasses that protected his sensitive eyes. She saw herself reflected in the black lenses, the painted-on features of her doll face looking startled and big.

"The deadly nightshade you slipped me wore off, Sally."

She tugged at her arm as she tried to pull away. "Let go!"

"You're not ready for so much excitement," Dr. Finkelstein explained evenly. He reminded himself that he had to be patient with new creations, like Sally. They were all curious in their first months of life, but that curiosity soon faded once they'd experienced a bit of freedom and gotten it out of their system. It was taking longer than expected with Sally, though.

I might have accidentally gotten some cat fur in her stuffing, he thought. *That could explain her relentless curiosity . . .*

Sally continued to tug uselessly as she insisted, "Yes I am!"

The doctor's electric wheelchair gave a buzzing drone as he mashed the button on it to spin around and drag her toward the castle. "You're coming with me," he growled. His hand was small but clawlike and strong as he pulled her along.

"No, I'm not!" She dug in her heels, but her cloth boots only slid over the smooth stone path. It wasn't fair! Every single creature in Halloween Town was celebrating the best night of the year, and she didn't want to sit locked in a dark tower, all alone, mending lab coats and polishing scalpels.

On impulse, Sally tugged on the dark blue thread that attached her right arm to the place just below her shoulder. The string unraveled from the cloth, and she fell back, separated from her own arm. She gasped, feeling un-whole.

The disembodied arm came free in Dr. Finkelstein's hands, causing him to tumble backward and fall out of his wheelchair.

Seeing her creator lying helplessly on the road, Sally stepped backward hesitantly. Could she just leave him and her arm behind?

The doctor's lips peeled back to show small sharp teeth. "Come back here, you foolish . . . Ow!"

Her disembodied right arm must have felt equally upset, because it formed a fist and pounded on Dr. Finkelstein's titanium scalp.

He sputtered. "Oh! Ow!"

Breathing hard, Sally blinked her doll eyes a few times and then turned and ran.

I'm sorry, arm. I'll find you again soon.

As Sally disappeared into the shadows, the din of the town's celebration grew louder. Monsters pressed in toward Jack, each trying to outdo the others to win the Pumpkin King's favor.

"Ohhh, Jack, you make wounds ooze and flesh crawl," the Undersea Gal moaned, leaning so close that her briny spray landed on his lapel. Her green scales and fanlike fins on the sides of her neck were slick. Her orange eyes blinked enticingly as her pointed blue fingernails reached out for the Pumpkin King.

Jack backed away slowly, holding out his bony hands beseechingly. "Thank you, thank you."

Almost moving as one amorphous blob, the crowd pressed even closer. Jack noticed the town's stone wall at his back, trapping him. Granted, a long-dead skeleton didn't need to breathe, but he certainly needed space. The townsfolk had been like this all night, applauding his every scare, oohing at his dancing. It was flattering, truly, so very kind of them . . . and yet stifling.

"Thank you very much," Jack said tightly, feeling more than a twinge of irritation. Why was he so bothered by the attention? He spent all year looking forward to Halloween. And he'd truly outdone himself that night, even finishing off the evening with his dramatic bonfire dance to give the townspeople one final surprise. But if he was honest, he hadn't felt *quite* the same enthusiasm that year as years before. In fact, something had been shifting every Halloween for the past few years. He'd thrown his heart and undead soul into making Halloween plans, but something had been missing. It all felt so *predictable*.

Couldn't a skeleton get a few minutes alone?

He glanced over his shoulder, eyeing the height of the stone wall. Could he make the jump?

Suddenly, a loud voice on a megaphone announced from the Town Square, "Hold it! We haven't given out the prizes yet!"

"Ooh!" cried the crowd, turning away from Jack.

Thank you, Mayor! Jack thought.

The lure of prizes was enough to draw the crowd back toward the Town Square. The Mayor, beaming proudly on his dais, hoisted a golden trophy over his shoulder.

"Our first award," he declared into his megaphone, "goes to the vampires for most blood drained in a single evening."

Polite applause filled the Town Square as the vampires glided on air up to the bandstand to accept their trophy.

While the crowd was distracted, Jack took a few steps away. He hoped no one in the crowd turned around and spotted him sneaking off.

"A frightening and honorable mention goes to the fabulous dark lagoon leeches." The Mayor's voice continued from the megaphone as Jack tiptoed away from the crowd, careful not to crunch loud dead leaves beneath his dry bones. Once he felt certain he was in the clear, he sighed in relief. The weight of the world seemed to slip off his shoulders.

Finally free, he ambled down the path away from the center of town and passed the trio of musicians that made up the Undead Ensemble, playing a morose serenade in front of the cemetery gates. He tossed a coin into the mouth of their saxophone.

"Nice work, Bone Daddy," the sax player said.

"Yeah, I guess so," Jack said over his shoulder as the graveyard gate rose for him. "Just like last year. And the year before that. And the year before that."

He wandered into the cemetery in a fog of melancholy, not certain why that year felt so different from years past.

CHAPTER THREE

0 DAYS TILL HALLOWEEN

ON THE OPPOSITE side of the cemetery, Sally rested her weary rag doll body against a tombstone as she gathered fallen leaves from the hole where her arm had been attached. After escaping from Dr. Finkelstein, she'd run straight to the cemetery, knowing that the ghosts that usually hovered close to their tombs would be celebrating and dancing with everyone else in the Town Square and she'd have the grounds to herself.

She listened to the Undead Ensemble play a

gloomy tune on the other side of the wall, then pause their music when the clink of a coin signaled someone tipping them, then take the song back up. How long could she manage without her right arm? Sooner or later, she'd have no choice but to return to Dr. Finkelstein's castle for it.

But not yet, she thought. She was determined to enjoy her freedom as long as she could.

The cemetery gate creaked open, and Sally gasped and scrambled to hide behind the tombstone. Someone else was there! She held her breath as she listened anxiously for the telltale whine of Dr. Finkelstein's electric wheelchair, but instead, light footsteps trod on the stone path, no louder than leaves scuffing in the wind.

The owner of the footsteps let out a burdened sigh.

Sally dared to peek over the top of the headstone and silenced another gasp. It was Jack Skellington! Why wasn't he at the party in the Town Square with everyone else? He was the guest of honor, after all, the same as he was every year. She had imagined that Jack would be so wrapped up in the celebration that he'd frolic the whole night long.

Yet on the greatest night of the year, here was the Pumpkin King, alone, like her.

Jack tipped his chin up and pondered the starless sky as he meandered through the cemetery. In the distance, the wind carried the raucous applause of the crowd celebrating the award winners back in town. Jack sighed to himself as he recalled that in years past, *he* had been the one leading them in cheers, his voice the loudest of all as he'd toasted with bubbly witch's brew. He'd recounted the night's best scares for the Winged Demon and the Corpse Kid and Mummy Boy, who'd listened in rapture. He'd danced until he feared he might die—*again*.

But this year, he couldn't shake an itchy-bone feeling that this was all the same and would be the same the next year and the next year and the next year . . .

As he passed a headstone shaped like a doghouse, he tapped his leg in a beckoning gesture. "Come on, Zero."

Jack's dog roused his ghostly body from its dirt-bed slumber and floated up until it hovered a few feet over the ground. As soon as Zero spotted Jack, his pumpkin nose glowed extra bright. He floated alongside Jack, panting happily.

Jack paced up the steepest of the cemetery hills, rubbing the sharp angle of his chinbone. What *was* this feeling gnawing at his bones? Why couldn't he be content reveling with the others as in years before? Not even Zero's soft glow cheered him up that night.

He leaned on a mausoleum topped by a demon statue and sighed. He wasn't himself that night, not at all. Everything just seemed so repetitive and dull.

He longed for something shiny. Something *new.*

Zero floated around Jack with his tongue lolling out.

Jack listened as the crowd partied in the distance. For a moment, he felt a mild stirring in his marrow as he remembered the night's most wonderful screams in the land of the living.

"Ah, Zero, you should have seen me tonight," he lamented. "I was at my most deliciously wicked."

He thought back fondly to the members of the sleepover party who had practically screamed off their braces when he'd popped out of one of their sleeping bags. He chuckled softly. For all his conflicted feelings, he had to admit that there was still something magical about All Hallows' Eve.

He climbed onto a tall tombstone, stretching to his full height, towering above Spiral Hill and the pumpkin patch beyond.

I'm the Pumpkin King, he thought fiercely. *That used to mean something. Maybe it still does.*

He curled his fingers into claws as he practiced

one of his more frightening faces. He'd perfected at least four hundred expressions of terror.

Zero followed along contentedly. The little dog loved it when Jack was feeling extra scary. He wagged his tail as Jack stepped nimbly from tombstone to tombstone.

I'm the foulest thing to ever come back from the dead, Jack thought as he raised his fists toward the moon, feeling the familiar stirring in his bones of a good thrill. *All cower when Jack, the Pumpkin King, stalks the shadows!*

Zero barked, excited. Jack danced his way from tombstone to tombstone, dreamily remembering the triumphant years of shrieks and screams. He twirled around the mournful angel statues standing guard at the cemetery gates and, with a pounce, flashed his most frightening face at them.

Their stone expressions remained unmoving.

Jack's limbs slowly sank. The sneer melted off his face. He'd felt a brief moment of the old joy caused by a good scare, but now the weariness was returning to his bones.

He slumped against a coffin and rested his chin on his hands.

Zero, concerned, nudged his friend with his glowing nose.

Jack sighed.

It was no use. He'd given his best performance that night, but it had still felt empty. He had to admit that he was simply growing tired of it all. The screams, the scares. What was it all *for*?

"I've done it all, Zero," he said. "Everything I set out to do. But there must be more than this. There simply must."

He waved his skeleton hand toward the pumpkin patch in the distance. At the edge of the patch, the woods began. It was a quiet, shadowy place, filled only with hooting owls and a strange wind. Jack had never ventured very far into the woods before, because there was no one there to scare except squirrels, and squirrels scared too easily; they'd scatter if a single nut fell.

But now he wondered: what was *beyond* the woods? Could there be a place where screams no longer echoed, where blood didn't run in the streets?

Somewhere . . . *else*?

"I've been the Pumpkin King for so many years," he mused. "Could it be time to relinquish the crown? Give it all up?"

Zero nuzzled Jack's bony scapula. The pumpkin-orange glow to the dog's nose dimmed at his seeing Jack so melancholic. He yipped, wanting another game of chase around the tombstones, but Jack was already walking along the unfurling slope of Spiral Hill, gazing off into the moonlight, wondering why no one else in Halloween Town understood the uneasy feeling that had settled deep in his marrow.

Hiding below the curving hill, Sally listened with fascination to Jack's sighs and his confession. She couldn't believe what she had heard.

The Pumpkin King? Wanting to give up his crown?

She touched the hole where her right arm should be. Jack felt like he was missing something; she knew that feeling all too well. Only in Jack's case, it wasn't a missing limb making him morose, but some broken part of his undead soul.

As Jack wandered down Spiral Hill and off toward the Hinterlands forest with Zero at his side, Sally rose from her hiding place and pressed a hand against her chest.

Jack had everything. She'd never dreamed that he would crave something more. But the truth was he felt trapped, just like her. Her prison was Dr. Finkelstein's tower, with its iron bars. Jack was a prisoner of his own success.

"Oh, Jack," she sighed, "I know how you feel."

CHAPTER FOUR

364 DAYS TILL HALLOWEEN

LONG AFTER Jack descended Spiral Hill and disappeared into the woods, Sally wandered the cemetery alone to think about what she'd heard. As unbelievable as it was to think that Jack, the Pumpkin King, felt trapped in their town, it made her realize just how badly she, too, longed for something more. Screams were all well and good, but what about love? Companionship? All she had ever known was Dr. Finkelstein's cold possessiveness.

She sank to her knees at the far end of the

cemetery, amid the swampy grass, where few other monsters went. Months earlier, she'd been wandering there and stumbled upon a sprig of wild nightshade. Ever since, whenever she'd been able to slip away from her creator, she had returned to that herb patch and carefully tended it. She'd even collected extra seeds from the witch sisters, who were careless with their potions and tossed their extra ingredients into the ditch outside their cottage. Now Sally had a poison garden bursting with henbane and witch hazel and a thriving crop of deadly nightshade. With her one remaining hand, she plucked a few leaves of nightshade and carefully tucked them into her dress.

She sighed to herself, pressing a hand where her missing arm should be, as she looked toward the forest one more time and thought of Jack.

One day, she thought, *maybe we'll both be free.*

But sadly, that day was not today.

Sally tried to be as silent as possible as she snuck back into Dr. Finkelstein's castle. Luckily, shoes made of soft cotton made it easy to be quiet. The castle's lanterns had been set low, and she hoped her creator was already in bed, fast asleep. She crept to the cupboard and hunted through the jars for the one labeled *Deadly Nightshade* and quickly stuffed in the herbs she'd harvested from her garden. She was just finishing when she heard the whine of Dr. Finkelstein's wheelchair.

She crammed the lid on the jar and shoved it back into the cupboard as lantern light flickered at the top of the long stone ramp that led to the top of the castle. Dr. Finkelstein rolled down to the bottom of the ramp.

"Sally!" The doctor's sharp voice pinned her to the wall. "You've come back."

She glanced over her shoulder at the cupboard, hoping he hadn't seen which jar she'd been holding.

"I had to," she said softly, blinking her doll eyes.

He gave a cold grin that pulled his thin lips back over his small teeth. "For this?"

He held up her right arm.

It looked sad and alone, just string and stuffing, and she felt guilty for having left it behind. The disembodied hand gave her a small sorrowful wave.

"Yes," she admitted.

The doctor laughed triumphantly. There was a reason he'd made Sally out of rags. His other creations were fearsome things: robots and reanimated corpses. They did his bidding, but they were brainless, heartless. He had made Sally because he had longed for someone to smile at him, to delight in cooking for him, to brighten up the sullen castle. But he'd made some misjudgment in her creation. He'd meant to make her soft through and through, but there was still something undeniably hard inside her, like a wooden button lodged in a sweater.

"Shall we, then?" The doctor motioned to the long curving ramp that led up to the castle's workrooms. Sighing, she started up the ramp. Her feet tried to object. They wanted to tear themselves off her body and run away back to the party in the Town Square or wander through the woods with Jack. But she forced them to obey.

Dr. Finkelstein, holding up the lantern to light their way, followed her in his chair.

The doctor's laboratory, which sat atop the castle's tower, had been built in the shape of a giant cauldron. It had always reminded Sally of the doctor's head: hard and round, riveted together with iron, with the inside reserved for brilliant but cruel work. In the laboratory, a disembodied hand floated in a clear jar of preservatives. Chemicals bubbled up from beakers as part of countless experiments. Sally glanced over the equipment with a chill. She hated the room, with its cold walls and smell of sulfur. This was the room where she'd come alive, slowly gaining consciousness out of the shadowy dark, blinking open her eyes.

Dr. Finkelstein strapped her back down on a table with leather binds, then threaded his needle. "That's twice this month you've slipped deadly nightshade into my tea and run off," he said as he painstakingly reattached her arm with thread.

She smiled in proud defiance. "Three times!"

He growled in annoyance, thrusting the needle dangerously close to her eye. "You're mine, you know. I made you with my own hands!"

She sighed as her gaze went to the rafters. "You can make other creations," she reasoned with him. "I'm restless. I can't help it."

For a moment, Dr. Finkelstein felt fatherly pity for her. He knew that hers was a lonely life, taking care of an old man in a wheelchair. He'd never much cared for the frenetic revelries of town, but he could see how a young and naive creature like Sally would be drawn to the festivities.

She would learn. All his creations learned in time.

"It's a phase, my dear," he said with slightly more sympathy, then bit off the thread as he finished attaching her arm. "It'll pass. We need to be patient, that's all."

"But I don't want to *be* patient!"

As the observatory roof cracked open with a rumble of machinery, Sally turned to look out at the starless sky over the woods.

Was Jack Skellington out there now? Did he still feel the same way? So . . . lost?

At least, she thought, *I refilled the jar of nightshade.*

The Hinterlands forest was a bleak, empty place. No leaves grew on the twisting trees. No grass crunched underfoot. There were no small animals to pounce on or bats overhead. And yet Jack found himself wandering deeper and deeper, farther than he ever had before. The sounds of town died down behind him until he could finally hear nothing but his own thoughts.

He was greatly troubled by a growing feeling of discontent. For the past few months, he'd been able to dismiss it. He told himself he was just overworked or maybe he'd eaten rancid meat when, really, a skeleton shouldn't eat anything at all. He'd thrown himself into Halloween preparations and pushed away those nagging feelings that something was *wrong*, something was *empty*. But now, with the holiday here and gone, there was nothing left to distract himself with. A light was shining brightly on those nagging thoughts, and he couldn't scare them back into the shadows.

Zero barked, wanting to play fetch.

"Not now, Zero," Jack said. "I'm not in the mood."

"Let me be boiled to death with melancholy," he thought morosely. That old ghoul Shakespeare sure knew how to put the feeling into words.

The ghost dog, panting persistently, continued to hover around him, and Jack relented.

"All right. Here you go, boy." He broke off one of his rib bones and tossed it deep into the shadows.

Zero found the bone in a hollow tree trunk and snatched it up happily. "Woof!"

Hours passed as Jack and Zero continued to meander through the forest. Jack clutched his skull with his thin fingers. He'd never given much thought to the Hinterlands, usually so empty and silent. But now he felt a whisper of magic. A curious wind rustled his bat bow tie. Hazy morning light rose in the east: had he really walked so far? Soon the sun grinned cruelly down on them like a jack-o'-lantern.

Jack yawned, blinking into the light, and asked Zero, "Where are we?"

That deep into the Hinterlands, the trees weren't gnarled and twisting as they had been at the edge of the forest, where Halloween Town ended. The sun cast a strange slanting light between the trees. The ground hummed with the promise of something different. The wind beckoned him toward a circular ring of trees.

He sniffed the air: was that the scent of candy?

"It's someplace *new,*" Jack realized with the stirring of interest.

Zero suddenly hung back, barking a low warning, as though he sensed possible danger amid the trees. But Jack ignored the dog.

"What is *this*?" Jack marveled.

Seven trees stood like sentinels around the perimeter of a clearing. Someone—or something—had carved bizarre but beautiful shapes into their trunks. The wind whispered secrets of old, making goose bumps erupt on his cold bones. The carvings were strange and colorful, almost like symbols . . . but symbols of what?

He touched his finger to his chin, considering.

One tree held a green four-leaved plant. Another showed a heart, though this heart wasn't pulsating and spurting blood, like the kind Jack was most familiar with. It seemed . . . *sweet*.

And there! Was that an egg, decorated festively with soft blues and yellows and pinks, the colors of spring? How peculiar! Next to it was a carving of a fat brown bird that made his mouth water, for some strange reason. The wind shifted, tasting of gravy.

Awed, Jack turned in a slow circle in the clearing. Zero barked uneasily again, but Jack was too entranced to notice the dog's hesitation.

Golden light, a color he'd never seen before, filtered in through the trees.

He felt a tingle throughout his body that he hadn't felt in decades. Life returning to his bones. A delicious curiosity he'd lost somewhere, somehow.

Whatever this was, it definitely wasn't Halloween Town.

He gasped as his gaze fell on the final tree.

The widest trunk was carved with a fantastical symbol unlike anything he'd ever seen. It appeared to be a bushy evergreen decorated with colorful balls and red-and-white-striped canes and a star at the top. There were even little people-shaped cookies that smelled like cinnamon. Jack had never seen anything like it.

So shimmery. So sparkly. So . . . *jolly*.

What did it mean? What were those colorful balls and those little cookie men? And the wrapped boxes tied with bows at the base of the tree?

Entranced, Jack drifted toward the magical

tree, with the wind at his back. Delighted, he realized that one of the colorful balls wasn't a ball at all, but a knob. Its shiny brass reflected his own grinning skeleton skull. Before he knew what he was doing, he reached out to the knob. His bones quaked with excitement. He'd never experienced anything like this!

The ball turned in his hand . . . and opened a door.

A realization struck him with delight: the carvings were secret doorways! Oh, what magical creature had done this? And why? And where did the door lead?

As he peered through the newly open doorway, his jawbone dropped in wonder.

Behind him, Zero hovered anxiously.

A frosty breeze twirled up from within the tree. The space inside the tree was dark but seemed somehow alive. Jack heard the tinkling of distant bells. The sound enticed him forward, into the dark . . .

Zero growled at the strange, strong wind that carried the smell of freshly fallen snow. Jack turned back toward his dog, concerned. But the wind had other ideas. It grew powerful enough to pull Jack back toward the open door.

Zero flew backward just in time to avoid the sudden gust, but Jack wasn't as fast.

The wind pulled Jack straight through the magical doorway and into the swirling darkness.

CHAPTER FIVE

364 DAYS TILL HALLOWEEN

BACK IN Halloween Town, none of the residents had noticed Jack's absence. The Pumpkin King's spindly three-story house was perched on one of the town's tallest hills, second in height only to Dr. Finkelstein's castle. A wrought iron gate in the shape of a pumpkin opened to a curving staircase, held up on precarious supports, that led to the front door. The house was much like Jack himself: angular and gaunt and somehow a little lonely even in the middle of a crowd.

Humming his favorite tune, the Mayor of Halloween Town steered his hearse over the cobblestone streets toward Jack's place. He wore his cheerful face now, and why not? It had truly been the best Halloween yet! But he couldn't let their recent success make them complacent. Oh, no. Now they had to top it for the next year—an even greater challenge, which meant they would need every minute of the next 364 days to plan and prepare. What a team—and, dare he say, friends?—they were, the Mayor and the Pumpkin King.

It was early, though not bright—the sun was never bright in Halloween Town—but the clouds were a lovely decomposed-skin shade of gray. The Mayor parked outside Jack's pumpkin gate and honked his horn, waking the snoring members of the Undead Ensemble, whose sallow faces said they'd been up all night playing their gloomy tunes.

Humming, he gathered up his rolls of papers and notes, then tipped his hat to the musicians. "Morning, gents!"

They blinked awake with some grumbles.

The Mayor climbed Jack's winding stairs with a happy jaunt. He tugged on the doorbell, an iron tarantula with fangs that was attached to the house by a thick string of webbing. The bell triggered a loud ring from somewhere inside the house, followed by an even louder recorded scream. At the announcement of a visitor, the doorknob's bloodshot eyeball blinked open to see who had come.

The Mayor rearranged his maps and charts while he hummed and waited.

A few minutes passed, and Jack didn't answer. The Mayor chuckled to himself, waved politely to the musicians who were hanging around outside the gate, and pulled the doorbell again.

The same recorded scream repeated.

That Jack. Probably still asleep. He deserves it today. But from now on, up early! the Mayor thought.

But the truth was he was beginning to get anxious. His neck tingled like it was going to start spinning his head around at any moment.

"Jack?" he called. "You home?"

There was still no answer. The Mayor felt a ticklish feeling, like crawling spiders, down his back. Why wasn't Jack answering?

His neck rotated his head to show his gloomy face. There was no hiding his anxiety now. He knocked harder in a panic before he remembered that the musicians were watching. He forced his cheerful face back in front so he could give them a wide grin, as though nothing was wrong.

"Jack?" he called back toward the house in a high pitch. "I've got the plans for next Halloween." He unrolled a diagram of bats, black cats, and jack-o'-lanterns and held it up to the eyeball doorknob. "I need to go over them with you so we can get started."

Jack still didn't come to the door. The Mayor didn't like this at all. No, not at all.

In his anxiousness, he accidentally dropped some of the rolls of Halloween plans, triggering another face change. He pleaded, pale-faced and gloomy, at the door. "Jack, please! I'm only an elected official here. I can't make decisions by myself!" He raised his megaphone to his lips. "Jack, answer me!"

He leaned back so far to shout into the megaphone that he lost his balance and tumbled backward, bumping his way painfully down the rickety stairs. "Ahh!" He rolled to a stop at the base of the pumpkin gate.

The Undead Ensemble, which had watched the whole production from the far side of the gate, shuffled closer.

"He's not home," the hulking accordion player said through the bars.

The Mayor wasn't sure which hurt more: his bruises or the nagging worry about Jack. He wailed, "Where is he?"

The sax player shrugged. "He hasn't been home all night."

"Ooh," the Mayor shrieked. His carefully rolled-up plans were crumpled. He'd dropped his megaphone somewhere. But those things could be replaced. Redrawn. *Jack* couldn't be replaced. Without Jack, there was no team. Even with two faces, he couldn't plan the best Halloween of all time on his own!

CHAPTER SIX

364 DAYS TILL HALLOWEEN

"W*HOA!"*

Snowflakes danced in the air around Jack as he tumbled down a swirling wintery vortex. The cold air nipped at his finger bones. It carried notes of peppermint and cinnamon. He could hear Zero barking in the distance, but Jack was somewhere else entirely now.

After a dizzying amount of time, his body rattled softly as he landed on a pile of icy white flakes. He was in a whole world of them. But what *were* they?

And what was the source of that delicious aroma? And that magical tinkling of bells? He pressed his hand to his skull until his vision began to steady.

What's this?

His eye sockets couldn't get any wider as his head twisted back and forth. He tried to take it all in at once. His jawbone clunked open from his sheer incredulity.

Another town!

Nestled in a white-covered valley sat an adorable magical village. Brightly colored strings of lights gave it a festive air. A cozy glow came from the decorated windows of each house and building. A delightful train chug-chugged in and out of equally delightful tunnels.

As much as he searched, Jack didn't see a single ghost. No impaled pumpkin heads on spikes. No yellow moonlight casting long shadows.

He'd never seen anything like this.

He gaped at the night sky. What were those twinkling things overhead? Why, they were *stars*!

There were no stars in Halloween Town. But here they shone down on the mystery town like someone had thrown handfuls of glitter onto a dark blue blanket.

Jack felt himself leaning forward, entranced by the marvelous spectacle, and suddenly leaned too far and toppled forward, unbalanced. His hand sank into the frosty stuff. So soft! Such a wonderful chill on his bones! He scooped up a handful of the cold substance, inspected it, and—why not?—took a bite. Intriguing. So fresh! Such zing! He untangled his long limbs and stood at full height on the hill to see better.

There!

Tiny people with pointed ears were skating on a frozen lake with a line of penguins.

And there!

Multicolored electric bulbs blinked on a decorated tree.

In his excitement, Jack lost his balance again and pinwheeled forward. The white stuff formed a wondrous kind of slide that zipped him down the mountain and straight into the center of town.

He popped his head up, then leapt to his feet, eager to inspect every single thing and unsure where to start. He grabbed a flake between his fingers to examine it.

It couldn't be real!

Every chimney and mailbox threatened to burst with charm. More fluffy white stuff covered the rooftops like cozy quilts. Twinkling lights surrounded each storefront and window.

"What's this? And this?" he cried. Someone had rolled the fluffy white stuff into three large balls of diminishing size, stacked them, and given the person-sized tower a hat and a carrot for a nose.

Oh, how clever! It looks like a man!

Jack heard high-pitched voices in song and tossed his head up. Some kind of vehicle was gliding smoothly his way. It wasn't a hearse. It wasn't a wagon pulled by a team of ghost horses.

Even more curiously, it appeared to be powered by a penguin jogging on a wheel in the rear where an engine should go. Three rosy-cheeked creatures rode on the vehicle and sang songs full of cheer as it skimmed along.

A worrisome thought entered Jack's skull. What if the sweet little creatures saw him? He didn't want to frighten them, at least not until he knew what they were, what this *place* was. He needed more time to study this intriguing new world. The person-shaped stack of round balls was about his height, so he thrust his bones right into the center of it and placed the top hat on his own head. Fortunately, his skull was the same glistening white color as the icy stuff.

He hadn't hid a moment too soon. In the next instant, more of the little creatures came his way, riding a large white bear with a little red-and-white-checkerboard saddle and a golden key in its side to engage its mechanical parts. Why, it was a toy! That explained why the bear hadn't gobbled up the little creatures.

I must be dreaming, Jack thought, then chuckled. *So be it. If I am, I never want to wake again!*

As soon as the coast was clear, he burst his way out of the cold statue and, keeping to the shadows, crept as quietly as a spider along the storefronts. More of the cheerful creatures passed by him, wearing big smiles as though they'd never been frightened a day in their lives. Hadn't they ever met the Creature Under the Stairs? The Undersea Gal? Not even a single wolfman?

From his hiding spot high on a streetlamp, he watched little people ball up handfuls of the fluffy flakes and toss them at one another. Ah, so it wasn't all merriment in this place after all: here was a fight. For a fleeting moment, Jack felt a pang of disappointment, but then he realized that instead of screaming and crying, everyone was laughing.

It wasn't a fight at all. It was *play.*

"Snowball coming!" one of the creatures yelled, tossing another ball.

Snow, Jack repeated silently to himself, testing out the strange word. That must be the name of the icy flakes. He felt as though he'd heard it before, maybe in the land of the living. Something about a monster called a yeti?

He toyed with a string of colorful lights and then sank back in dreamy reverie against one of the little houses. This one had a wreath circling the round front-door window, and to his delight, when he peeked inside, he saw a rosy-nosed couple kissing beneath mistletoe.

Delightful!

Jack crept along the same house until he reached another window. A wonderful sugary scent wafted his way. He peeked inside. There was a warm fire in the fireplace There were no spiderwebs in the corners of the room. He didn't smell a trace of worm's wort. Instead of dead rodents nailed to the walls, there were photographs of *happy* people. While a penguin reclined on a pillow in front of the roaring fireplace, a gray-haired woman Jack assumed must be a witch, judging by her pointed boots, was kindly reading stories to two small children—not a very witchy thing to do at all!

He hurried to the next house. He saw no poison in the cupboard. No rotten cabbage on the dinner table. The residents of this home had brought a little green tree *inside* the house. What strange beasts! They were draping the small tree with strings of colored lights and miniature ornaments. But why? How would twinkling lights scare anyone? Were they going to strangle one another with the wires?

It's almost like they don't want *to scare anyone,* he mused. *It's like they'd rather have fun. Why, that's it exactly! Fun!*

With a happy cry, Jack leapt onto a windowsill and then onto the neighboring house's roof, where he scrambled to the very top and marveled at the stars overhead. What was this feeling in his bones? He'd never felt so light. He wanted to twirl and dance and sashay with the snow itself.

"I wanted something new," he whispered to himself. "Is this what I wished for?"

He heard soft snores and swung down from the rooftop to peek inside another window. As his curiosity got the better of him, he quietly unlatched it and snuck inside. It was a charming little bedroom with tiny tots asleep in bunk beds and dresser drawers. He'd spent a lifetime learning how to terrify small sleeping children, but for some reason, he didn't feel inclined to frighten these sleeping angels. How deeply they slumbered! He took a peek under the bed and found only tiny shoes, no monsters at all.

What would all his friends in Halloween Town think of *this*?

Jack tiptoed to the next bedroom and bent down to inspect the handful of children tucked beneath the covers. They smiled in their sleep, as though they were having *pleasant* dreams instead of nightmares. Did these children even know about vampires? Had they never awoken to a cackling devil looming over them?

They were so vulnerable tucked in their beds that it would almost be too easy to terrorize them. But scaring was the farthest thing from Jack's mind. He didn't want their screams—he wanted their smiles!

What an extraordinary realization!

Sighing from the dreamy feeling of having discovered something new within himself, he gave one of the creatures a gentle pat and then slunk back out the bedroom window.

The sleeping tot jolted awake, but Jack was already gone.

The skeleton danced his way onto the next rooftop, which appeared to belong to some sort of factory. Through frosted windows he watched the silhouettes of little creatures merrily making rocking horses and toy trains.

"Incredible," Jack whispered.

He hooked the curved handle of an umbrella he'd taken from the snow-shaped man onto a garland and slid his way across town, marveling at a pie display in a bakery window. Then he dropped onto a merry-go-round that had models of penguins and bears bobbing up and down on poles instead of corpse horses, like all the rides in Halloween Town. He let the ride spin him around, his head dizzily full of wondrous new thoughts. For so long, he'd felt an emptiness deep in his bones.

Was *this* what had been missing in his life? Snow? Teddy bears? *Pie?*

He twirled off the merry-go-round, landed on the town's jolly train, and rode it until the very second it disappeared into a tunnel. He jumped off at the last minute onto a sled that slid him back down the mountain into the center of town. He jumped off that a little too fast and, without watching where he was going, collided with a tall red-and-white-striped pole and fell backward into the snow.

Pressing a hand to his aching skull, he squinted up at the sign he'd run into.

"Christmas Town? Hmm . . ."

His mind turned back to that strange clearing in the Hinterlands and the trees with their odd symbols that were actually doors. One had been a jack-o'-lantern shape, which logically must lead to Halloween Town. He'd opened the door in the shape of the decorated little tree and ended up here, in Christmas Town. That meant there must be equally strange worlds through *all* the doors . . .

A train whistle blasted. Somewhere nearby, hinges groaned as a giant door flew open on the largest house in town. With a gasp, Jack hid his thin body behind the town sign, peeking out cautiously.

A deep voice rumbled out into the night: *"Ho-ho-ho!"*

Along with the voice, a gigantic shadow stretched onto the hills.

Ah, here was something familiar to Jack! A hulking shadow. A deep cackle—though it wasn't exactly sinister. Whoever this new person was, he was much larger and more frightening than the town's cheerful little creatures.

Maybe this was the leader of this . . . Christmas Town?

"Hmmm." Jack narrowed his eyes, wondering.

This *ho-ho-ho*ing shadow might not like having another king in town.

CHAPTER SEVEN

364 DAYS TILL HALLOWEEN

WORD OF JACK'S disappearance spread quickly throughout Halloween Town, carried like dried fall leaves on miasmic air. It wasn't long before every resident had heard the troubling news. They crawled out of their houses and caves and banged on the door of Town Hall, demanding answers. Even the vampires dared to venture outside during the day under the protection of heavy black umbrellas.

"This has never happened before!" cried the

Clown with the Tear-Away Face, slapping his hands against his painted cheeks.

"It's suspicious," the big witch with the mossy hair said.

"It's peculiar," added her small sister.

A vampire dramatically clutched his chest with one hand while holding an umbrella with the other and gasped in unison with his companion, "It is *scary*!"

"Stand aside!" the Mayor said, using as much authority as he could muster to push through the crowd. He'd worn his grim face ever since leaving Jack's house and feared he'd never have a reason to switch to the smiling one again. In his hurry, he accidentally shoved the Wolfman, who whirled on him with a warning growl, but the Mayor was so distraught that he hardly noticed.

"Coming through," he ordered as he maneuvered his topsy-turvy body up a ladder to the top of his hearse, where he promptly lost his balance and fell. He managed to right himself and took ahold of his megaphone. He announced into it, "We've got to find Jack. There's only three hundred sixty-five days left till next Halloween!"

"Three sixty-four," growled the Wolfman, who was still irritated.

The Mayor moaned. It was true. Now he was even losing track of the days. They were going to run out of time to plan the most frightening Halloween ever.

The concerned residents fretted.

"Is there anywhere we've forgotten to check?" the Mayor pleaded.

"I looked in every mausoleum," the Clown with the Tear-Away Face swore, rocking tightly back and forth on his tiny unicycle.

"We opened the sarcophagi," the witches said in unison.

Mr. Hyde shambled up in his dented top hat and green cloak. One of his feet was stuck in a pumpkin; in his worry, he hadn't even stopped to free it. "I tromped through the pumpkin patch. Nothing!"

One of the vampires who had won the award for most blood drained added in his rasping voice, "I peeked behind the Cyclops' eye!" When the witch sisters cackled with a disbelieving sneer, he insisted, "I did!" He pulled out his own eyeball for emphasis before letting it snap back into place. He blinked a few times to make sure it had settled, and then sighed, "But he wasn't there."

The Mayor nodded decisively. "It's time to sound the alarms!"

Mummy Boy climbed up on the hearse with considerably more agility than the Mayor had and began to crank the tail of the black-cat siren, which let out a shrieking wail of alarm.

High up in the castle, Sally heard the alarm as she was in the midst of preparing Dr. Finkelstein's soup. She leaned out the kitchen window, trying to figure out why everyone was gathered. Stuck in the castle, she hadn't heard the news of Jack's disappearance. What did the alarm signal? Had a vampire spent too long in the sun? Was a plague of locusts swarming on the pumpkin patch? She had the same churned-up feeling in her stomach she'd had the night before, when she'd listened to Jack's musings in the graveyard.

Please, don't let anything have happened to Jack . . .

There was only one thing to do. Good thing she'd gathered that extra nightshade.

She cocked her head to listen to the creaks and moans of the castle. She didn't hear any sign of Dr. Finkelstein's wheelchair. He was working on a new experiment in his laboratory—something perplexing that involved the preserved hand in a jar—and it had kept him so busy that he'd skipped breakfast.

Now it was almost lunchtime, which meant the doctor must be starving—so starving he might not look too closely at what he was served . . .

She threw open the cupboard, hunting through the jars for the nightshade. One had to be careful when brewing with poisons. Too little would only give the victim a bout of nausea. Too much and they'd die. Sally didn't want to kill Dr. Finkelstein; he'd made her, after all, and she had a soft spot for lonely old recluses. She only wanted to put him to sleep. Besides, if he threw up from a botched poisoning, *she'd* be the one to have to clean it up.

She carefully measured a portion of nightshade and mixed it into the soup that was simmering in the kitchen cauldron. A noxious burst of steam rose from the pot, and she reeled backward, pinching her nose, as she waved away the vile odor. One whiff of this telltale scent and Dr. Finkelstein would know exactly what she was up to.

She grabbed a jar off the kitchen shelf and unscrewed the cap. "Frog's breath will overpower any odor."

At her prodding, the frog inside the jar stretched himself and gave a nice ripe belch into the stew. She pinched her nose again against the smell. It was so pungent that it made her head spin, and she coughed, dizzy, as she set down the jar and stumbled her way across the kitchen to the cabinet where she kept her ingredients.

"Bitter!" She opened the cabinet door with a groan of hinges as she continued to cough. "Worm's wort," she wheezed. "Where's that worm's wort?" She tossed jars and canisters over her head until she found it at last.

Though worm's wort was precious, it was worth using the last of her stores of it to mask the traces of poison the frog's breath didn't quite hide. Besides, Dr. Finkelstein adored worm's wort. Surely he'd suck down the soup without giving it a second thought.

Somewhere overhead, a door squeaked open.

"Sally?" Dr. Finkelstein's sharp voice snaked down the spiral ramp. "Is that soup ready yet?"

From three stories down she could practically hear his stomach growling.

She poured the worm's wort into the soup at arm's length, not wanting to breathe in the vapors. Then she cocked her head, pleased. "Coming!"

She ladled out a bowl and carefully carried it up the long ramp to his laboratory. Dr. Finkelstein was stooped over his worktable, deep in thought. X-rays of various body parts were set out next to the preserved hand in a jar.

"Hmm," he mused to himself, confused by his latest experiment. He opened his skullcap and gave his brain a nice juicy scratch, waking up the synapses, then closed his head with a squeak of its hinges.

"Lunch," Sally announced proudly.

"Ah." He moved aside his equipment and wheeled his chair closer to the table. "What's that?"

Sally plastered an innocent smile on her face as the doctor leaned forward to give the stew a deep inhale. His stomach rumbled audibly.

He beamed. "Worm's wort! Mmmm." He clutched the spoon and raised it to his thin, quivering lips. Sally leaned forward with her hands clasped and her eyes big, silently urging him to take a sip. But a second before he touched the greenish brine to his lips, he stopped. All traces of excitement fell off his face. Behind his black glasses, his tiny eyes narrowed. "And *frog's breath*?"

Sally blinked her big eyes extra dramatically, feigning confusion. "Well, what's wrong? I thought you liked frog's breath."

Dr. Finkelstein waved the spoon in the air as he squinted at her from behind his glasses. "Nothing's more suspicious than frog's breath."

He sighed to himself. Here he'd gone and taken a chance with Sally. Made something soft, something pliable. But there was a scheming brain in her head behind that stitched-on smile.

He slid the bowl toward her and demanded, "Until you taste it, I won't swallow a spoonful."

Sally immediately huffed, "I'm not hungry." She was an above-average actress, and she enjoyed putting on the little display. She threw up her arms like a petulant child, intentionally knocking the spoon out of his hand. It clattered to the floor beneath the table, and she cried, "Oops!"

Bending down, she quietly kicked the spoon farther under the table and, while out of his sight, pulled a strainer spoon from her wool sock, where she'd tucked it before going to the laboratory.

"You want me to starve?" Dr. Finkelstein growled as he waited. "An old man like me who hardly has strength as it is? Me, to whom you owe your very life?"

Sally popped up, grinning from ear to ear. She was relieved that she'd had the idea to bring along the strainer spoon just in case.

"Oh, don't be silly," she said, taking the bowl of soup. She held it high over his head, grateful again that he couldn't stand up from his chair, so he couldn't see that when she dipped in her strainer spoon, the greenish brew simply drained out of its holes immediately.

She tipped the empty spoon toward her lips and pretended to slurp a big sip. "Mmm. See? Scrumptious!"

Sally slid the bowl back to Dr. Finkelstein. Satisfied by her demonstration, he embraced it ravenously, drinking directly from the bowl. Worm's wort *was* his favorite, and Sally hadn't made it for ages. Good old Sally. He had been needlessly paranoid to think she would try to trick him again.

He slurped down the entire bowl, licking his thin lips with gusto.

He gave a satisfied belch, and Sally grinned wider, clutching her hands together against her chest.

Now she just had to wait . . . and hope she hadn't accidentally killed her creator.

CHAPTER EIGHT

363 DAYS TILL HALLOWEEN

THE MONSTERS OF Halloween Town fretted and fussed over Jack's disappearance until every inch of town had been thoroughly scoured from top to bottom. Every coffin was excavated, and every sewer was tromped through, but there was simply no sign of the Pumpkin King. The Mayor's head had rotated between his two faces so quickly that eventually he collapsed in dizzy despair on top of his hearse. One by one, the other residents had slunk back to the Town Square, equally despondent. Their raison d'être was planning scares for Halloween night—and they couldn't do that without Jack!

"Did anyone think to dredge the lake?" the Mayor wailed.

One of the vampires, languishing under his umbrella, moaned, "This morning."

The air held a fetid, heavy feeling, like swamp water. If Jack didn't return, it would mean doom for Halloween Town. They'd be lucky if they could scare a five-year-old in a princess costume.

Just as their despair seemed interminable, a small bark sounded outside the town gates.

The big witch perked up and prodded her sister. "Hear that?" She took off her conical hat and used it like an ear trumpet.

"What?" the little witch growled.

"Shhh!" hissed the first.

The witch wasn't the only one who had heard. Several of the monsters roused themselves and sat up, listening intently.

The *yip* came again.

The Mayor's head rotated to his smiling side with a swift *creaaak* of his neck.

"Zero!" one of the vampires exclaimed, so excited that he almost dropped his umbrella, which would have reduced him to slime and ash.

The gathering participants scrambled to their feet as though a bolt of lightning had struck the hearse and shot electricity through them all.

Could it be? Was Jack really back?

The gatekeeper raised the creaky gate. Even the buildings of Halloween Town seemed excited to see the return of the Pumpkin King, their lights flickering in celebration.

Jack swept through the gates riding atop a peculiar contraption painted in bright greens and reds. It appeared to be a small car pulling a red cart filled with a mysterious bundle tied up in red-and-white string. He tipped his chin high, and he wore driving goggles, as though he'd come from a vast distance at great speed. Yipping in excitement, Zero floated ahead of him on a cloud of frosty air.

Cheers echoed off the town's angular rooftops and walls.

"Jack's back!" the Corpse Kid, the Winged Demon, and Mummy Boy cried out as they tripped their way toward the gate.

The Mayor pressed his hands against his happy face, barely able to keep his excitement from oozing out his pores. He grinned down at Jack widely. "Where have you been?"

Jack sat upright in the driver's seat of the colorful contraption. He ripped off the driving goggles. Beneath them, his hollow eye sockets glistened with the promise of something *new*. That was Jack, always full of surprises. Who else would come back from the dead smelling so oddly of cinnamon?

Jack hoisted a finger in the air. "Call a town meeting and I'll tell everyone all about it."

The Mayor wasn't sure what to think of Jack's secrecy. His face rotated back to the worried side. "When?"

Jack threw his hands into the air, no longer able to rein in his excitement. "Immediately!"

Sally chuckled to herself as she crept into the laboratory to check on Dr. Finkelstein. Her nightshade-laced soup had worked again. To her relief, the doctor was fast asleep at his worktable. His thin lips smacked softly as he snored hard enough to ruffle the X-rays spread on the table. She found a blanket on the bench and placed it tenderly over his shoulders, giving him a gentle pat.

Sweet nightmares, she thought.

From the open window, she heard Town Hall's bell ringing and the Mayor making an announcement through his megaphone: "Town meeting! Town meeting!"

Sally ran to the window and looked down. The Mayor was cruising in his hearse along every winding street in Halloween Town, calling out in his most authoritative voice, "Town meeting tonight!"

Town Hall's bell continued to clang to signal the urgency.

Anxious, Sally toyed with the thick blue stitching at her neck.

What's this town meeting about? she wondered.

She hurried down the spiral ramp and slipped out of the castle, then tottered down the hill toward Town Hall, where a crowd was already gathering. Night had fallen quickly. The vampires lowered their umbrellas, basking in the cool, harmless dark. The town's small pack of children laughed and skipped up the stairs into the auditorium.

Narrowly avoiding a collision with one of the witch sisters flying in on her broom, Sally joined the crowd filing into the auditorium, but she hung back in the shadows once inside. These were her neighbors and friends, yet they'd always treated her a little differently. Instead of fangs and claws, she had thread and old leaves for stuffing. None of the other monsters quite knew what to do with her.

Inside the auditorium, there was a commotion as everyone fought for the best seats in the house. The stage was empty except for the drab curtain, which was mysteriously closed now, and an upright coffin used as a podium.

Honking his toy horn, the Clown with the Tear-Away Face wheeled a little too close, almost knocking Sally over, then giggled as he backed up and zoomed toward the front of the room.

Sally hunted for a seat, but they all had been filled. Just when she worried she'd have to stand outside, a branch tapped on her shoulder. The Hanging Tree loomed behind her in the back of the room with its dangling noosed skeletons. One of the skeletons pointed a bony finger to the tree's wide limb.

Sally thanked them and hoisted up her skirt so she could climb onto the branch between the

Hanging Men's ropes. She gave the tree a sweet pat. It was the best seat in town.

She was arranging her skirt when the auditorium's side door swung open and Jack strode out of the wings, beaming as he went to stand behind the podium. Before the crowd could even begin to cheer, Jack said, "Listen, everyone!"

The lights dimmed. The auditorium hummed with anticipation as everyone quickly finished settling into their seats and at last grew quiet.

"I want to tell you about Christmas Town," Jack announced.

In the rear of the auditorium, the Mayor switched on the spotlight, which startled the bats that had been roosting there. They took wing into the rafters. The Mayor swung the light to the front of the stage and centered it on Jack.

Curious murmurs ran through the crowd. Besides Halloween Town and the land of the living, there were no other towns. Was Jack talking about the vast, empty Hinterlands? Or the cornfields beyond the gate? Or that reeking pit Oogie Boogie called home?

Jack adjusted his bat bow tie and cleared his throat. "There is a place, my friends, that is positively magical! It's indescribable, but I shall try my best. First, I must ask you to suspend your disbelief. What I am about to tell you will stretch your imagination, but it's true. I've been there! Here, I'll show you."

With a flourish, he tugged a dangling chain, and the dusty curtains swept open to reveal a colorful vignette unlike anything anyone had ever seen.

"Oooh," the crowd gasped, leaning in, as the colorful lights glittered in their eyes.

Onstage, a skeletal tree with skimpy branches was draped with a string of electric lights and shiny colorful balls. It sat next to the mystery sack Jack had brought back with him.

Sally leaned forward, entranced by the lights, and almost fell off the tree limb.

The crowd watched in fascination as Jack opened the sack and took out a box wrapped in paper.

"This box is called a present," he explained, holding it up for everyone to see.

The Devil jumped up from his seat, asking what the box was made of.

The Wolfman immediately wanted to know if it was locked.

The Harlequin Demon elbowed them both aside with his sharp feathered arms and rasped, "What's in the box, Jack? Pestilence? Disease?"

The Wolfman and the Devil clapped their hands, forgetting the demon's roughhousing. "How delightful!"

From the stage, Jack watched the crowd's reaction and hesitated. They didn't quite understand what he was trying to tell them about Christmas, but that was okay. He'd try again.

"It isn't that kind of a box," he explained. "You see, the point is that it's wrapped in this whimsical paper and tied up with a bow . . ."

The witch sisters flew on their brooms to the stage for a closer look and shrieked, "A *bow*? Why? What's in the box, Jack?"

Jack explained patiently, "That's the whole point of the box. No one knows what's inside. It's a surprise."

The Clown with the Tear-Away Face scratched his red nose. "Maybe it's a toad."

"Or a snake," the Creature Under the Stairs offered. "Judging by the size."

The Undersea Gal, who had been clinging to the rafters and dripping clammy water on everyone, hung upside down to offer her own guess. "Ooh! Is it the severed head from the lake?"

Jack set down the box on a stool. He pressed his bony fingers to his skull, massaging away the start of a headache.

"Listen, my friends," he said, trying again. "Pay attention. Christmas Town isn't filled with toads or snakes or severed heads. Hmm . . . allow me to try another example."

He dug through the sack, pushing past a giant letter *C* he'd taken from the Christmas Town sign, and picked up a large red sock rimmed with white fur.

He held up the sock with a flourish. "In Christmas Town, they hang these giant socks above the fireplace—"

"Where's the foot?" Mr. Hyde said, walking onto the stage and interrupting Jack's presentation as he tried to peer into the sock. "Awfully large sock. Is the foot still inside? Has it turned gangrenous yet?" Several miniature versions of Mr. Hyde, hidden beneath his hat like nesting dolls, popped up with their own questions about the sock.

Jack frowned as he answered the Mr. Hydes of diminishing size: "There's no foot. The creatures of Christmas Town fill these giant socks with *candy*. Or *toys*."

The monstrous children in the audience jumped up at the mention of toys.

Mummy Boy bounced up and down. "What kind of toys? Rotten rats?"

"Do they stink?" the Corpse Kid asked.

"I get it now!" said the Winged Demon. "They're scary toys! The surprise is that they explode in the faces of boys and girls who open the box!"

The crowd erupted in applause at the idea of exploding trick presents that reeked of gangrene.

The Mayor, sensing the crowd's enthusiasm, cleared his throat and called out from the back of the room, "What fun! I'm officially on board with this Christmas idea. Especially the severed heads. I'll rework our scare plans immediately." He was eager to remind everyone that he and Jack were a team when it came to holiday planning. In his excitement, he knocked into the spotlight, which angled all around the room.

The crowd was chattering about the naughty surprises they could hide in boxes when Jack loudly rapped his bare knuckles on the podium. "Everyone, wait! If I may beg your attention once more . . . I don't think you quite understand what I'm trying to say."

But the crowd was buzzing so loudly they hardly heard him. The children at the front of the room were already taking off their socks and filling them with ticks plucked from behind their ears.

Jack sighed. None of them understood. But really, how could they? He didn't blame them for their confusion. Would he have understood before he'd seen it with his own eyes?

"I need to put it in terms they'll understand," he mused to himself, and racked his shriveled brain for anything about Christmas Town they could relate to. There had to be something moderately frightening about the place . . .

His eyes fell on Halloween Town's demonic little trick-or-treaters, Lock, Shock, and Barrel, who were bouncing up and down on a bench. They were Oogie Boogie's trio of troublemakers. Oogie Boogie himself hadn't come to the meeting; he rarely left his creepy-crawly lair except on Halloween night itself, when he rivaled Jack for best scares.

That *ho-ho-ho*ing person's shadow stretching over the snow in Christmas Town had reminded Jack of Oogie Boogie . . .

That's it! he thought.

Offering his most terrifying Pumpkin King leer, Jack leaned over the podium. "I've saved the best for last," he growled. Immediately, the crowd fell into a hush, and he continued, "Christmas Town is ruled by a terrible king. His arms are thick as tree trunks. His voice is deep as the mud at the bottom of the lake."

"Ooh," Mummy Boy said with a shiver.

Jack grinned as he strode into the audience. Now he had them. All it took was a little Pumpkin King flair, and at that he had no rival.

As he poked the Melting Man in his gooey nose, Jack said, "The Christmas King flies through the night not on a broom but on a cart pulled by horned beasts, and casts a reign of terror upon boys and girls on December twenty-fifth!"

He turned to Behemoth and pulled out his long tongue. "He dresses in bloodred garments!"

"Who is he, Jack?" the smaller of the witch sisters cried. Both witches clutched their green hands together, enthralled by the idea of a dashingly wicked king who shared their love of flying.

"His name," Jack announced dramatically as he returned to the stage, "is Sandy Claws." He curled his bony fingers in the shape of claws as he gave his best spine-tingling cackle.

The crowd shrieked and clapped.

Sally, perched in the tree, clapped her cloth hands even though they made little sound. It was wonderful to see Jack excited about something after what she'd overheard in the cemetery, and this Sandy Claws and Christmas thing, with its exploding presents and severed feet, sounded perfectly lovely. At the same time, she detected a strange tone in Jack's voice, like he was holding something back. She cocked her head, wondering. Was this what Jack had been talking about in the cemetery? Would this Christmas thing fill the emptiness in his bones?

As the applause continued, Jack disappeared behind the curtain. The moment he was alone in the wings, hidden behind the curtain, his grin faded.

He heaved a great sigh. It would take more than twinkling lights and stockings to make the others understand the magic of Christmas. Alone in the backstage shadows, he picked up a snow globe and gave it a gentle shake. The white flakes inside swirled around a snowman in a top hat. Jack felt a magical tingle inside his bones, reassuring him. He could almost taste plum pudding.

He'd figure out how to share Christmas with them. There simply had to be a way. At least they were excited. Their bloodshot eyes had gleamed in wonder. Their cheers still echoed in the auditorium's rafters.

But they hadn't really understood.

"Oh, well," he mused to himself.

It was a start.

CHAPTER NINE

358 DAYS TILL HALLOWEEN

THE SLIVERED MOON was high. In the darkness, an owl hooted. Every resident of Halloween Town was tucked into bed, sweet nightmares haunting their slumber, every light switched off except for the blazing bulbs in the turret window of Jack Skellington's spindly house.

Jack sat upright in his creaky wrought iron bed, where crimson-eyed gargoyles perched on the bedposts as he read. A fire crackled in the hearth nearby. A scraggly evergreen tree, hung with a string of lights and a few colorful balls, loomed over the bed. Jack had searched high and low in the pumpkin patches for a fat, full evergreen like the ones that could be found on every corner in Christmas Town. But like most of Halloween Town's vegetation, the trees there were anemic and wan; Jack supposed the ever-present fog obscuring the sun had something to do with it. And perhaps the acid rain.

Not far away, Zero slumbered contentedly in his dog bed, clutching an oversized candy cane in his ghostly jaw.

For the better part of a week, ever since his Town Hall meeting, Jack had paced the cold floors of his turreted rooms, trying to get to the bottom of what made Christmas so magical so he could adequately convey that feeling to his fellow citizens.

His walls reeked of burned gingerbread: his attempt at baking cookies hadn't gone well. In fact, *none* of his attempts to re-create Christmas cheer had succeeded. After his baking disaster, he'd visited Halloween Town's library, where ghostly librarians haunting the stacks helped him hunt down every source on Christmas he could lay his bones on. He'd found a guidebook to something called yuletide; tales from the elves' workshop; a fat history book of bows; and a bizarre account of a red-nosed reindeer.

The nose wasn't even bloody—it was simply red!

Now, as the fire crackled, Jack sighed and set down a worn copy of *A Christmas Carol*. The book had seemed promising at first—there were plenty of ghosts and rattling chains to entice the townsfolks' interest—but ultimately, Mr. Dickens' story didn't unlock the mystery of Christmas. It ended with Mr. Scrooge, the only interesting fellow in the story, giving away his life savings to a dull do-gooder employee. What a terrible message.

Jack slammed the book closed and let his gaze wander around the Christmas trinkets he'd brought back with him in the snowmobile.

How do I capture holiday magic like snow in a snow globe? he wondered.

The evergreen garlands he'd strung up around his bedroom offered no answers. Neither did the black widow spider who lived in his chimney and had spun his strings of Christmas lights into a colorful web.

"There's got to be a logical way to explain this Christmas thing," Jack mused.

The precariously balanced stack of books from the library was a dead end, but then he recalled a book one of the townsfolk, the rag doll named Sally, had once given him on behalf of Dr. Finkelstein.

The book was titled *The Scientific Method.*

"Hmm . . ." Jack grabbed the book and flipped to the first page, curious. The smell of oleander and worm's wort wafted up from the crisp pages, summoning thoughts of Sally toiling away in Dr. Finkelstein's cold laboratory.

He was starting to have an idea.

Maybe if he couldn't capture Christmas in words, he could take a lesson from Halloween Town's evil doctor and explain the holiday through science.

The following day, in his hillside castle, Dr. Finkelstein clutched an ice pack to his aching skullcap. He moaned like a dog. Poisoning by *Atropa belladonna*, otherwise known as deadly nightshade, resulted in an intense sensitivity to light and a throbbing headache that forced him to squint painfully behind his dark glasses.

He'd woken that morning passed out on his laboratory desk next to his bowl of soup. That Sally! She'd tricked him again! He had called for his assistant, Igor, to fetch his binoculars so he could search the town from the window for signs of her. Igor had limped in with the heavy iron lenses, and the doctor had spied down at the goings-on until he finally spotted his rag doll gardening amid the weeds in the cemetery.

Igor had dragged her back, kicking and screaming, by her long red hair.

Now, scowling, Dr. Finkelstein glowered at Sally as she sat morosely in her cell, which was mostly bare except for a few spare items and a rusty metal cot.

"You've poisoned me for the last time, you wretched girl," the doctor growled.

Sally sighed and rested her cheek on her hand.

Still clutching the ice pack to his skull, the doctor pushed the heavy door of the cell closed, nodding to himself in satisfaction as the bolt fell down with a heavy thunk.

Try getting out now, he thought.

Sally's disobedience was getting out of hand. If Igor hadn't caught her, she might never have returned. Maybe it had been a mistake to make her out of fabric and thread. She was too soft, too tenderhearted. He had thought that by making Sally his opposite, he would have a complementary companion who excelled at cooking and cleaning and all the domestic things he loathed. And while Sally *did* make tasty worm's wort stew, she was also headstrong, curious, and utterly insolent in her childlike wonder.

Next time, he'd create a companion closer to his own image.

The doorbell rang loudly, and Dr. Finkelstein cringed as the bell's chime reverberated in his aching skull.

"Oh, my head . . ." he moaned.

He fumbled with his wheelchair's controls until he steered himself to the top of the tower's ramp, where he could peer down into the foyer below.

"The door is open!" he called, adjusting the ice pack.

The castle's wooden door creaked wide to reveal Jack, wearing a freshly starched bat bow tie and clutching a black medical bag in one hand. "Hello?"

"Jack Skellington!" Dr. Finkelstein exclaimed. He was always pleased to see Jack, one of the few residents of Halloween Town who demonstrated that they possessed a brain—unlike that ridiculous Mayor, who couldn't even decide which face to wear from one minute to the next. "Up here, my boy!"

Jack marched up the ramp with enthusiasm. "Doctor, I need to borrow some equipment."

Dr. Finkelstein beamed. Jack must be up to something good. It had been a long time since anyone had come to him for advice. "Is that so? Whatever for?"

"I'm conducting a series of experiments," Jack explained.

"How perfectly marvelous." Dr. Finkelstein wheeled closer to the top of the ramp as Jack climbed the final incline, toting his medical bag. Now here was a strapping young skeleton who understood the value of science, not like that wretched rag doll, with her wide eyes hungry to take in everything at once without the proper procedures and protocols.

"Curiosity killed the cat, you know," the doctor warned him.

"I know," Jack agreed.

"Come on into the lab," the doctor said, pressing his wheelchair controls to spin himself around. The ice pack was beginning to clear his head of the nightshade's effects, and he was feeling much more himself. "We'll get you all fixed up."

As Jack followed Dr. Finkelstein to his laboratory, Sally sat up in her bed in surprise at the familiar voice. What was Jack Skellington doing there? She pressed herself against her cell door to overhear their conversation.

"Hmm," Sally thought aloud. "Experiments?"

CHAPTER TEN

357 DAYS TILL HALLOWEEN

"ZERO, I'M HOME!"

The ghostly dog blinked awake, his nose glowing brighter at the sound of Jack's voice. Jack climbed up the spiral staircase, eager to get to work. His visit to Dr. Finkelstein's castle had been a definitive success. He'd managed to borrow every piece of equipment *The Scientific Method* mentioned—a microscope, test tubes, beakers, and burners—though it was a shame he hadn't run into Sally while at the castle. He'd have liked to thank her for the book, which had given him the idea to find the answer to this Christmas thing through tried-and-true methods.

The Scientific Method laid out seven steps any good scientist should take. The first step was to identify the question in need of answering. Well, that was simple enough: *What is the magic of Christmas?* Jack felt a delicious frosty chill in his bones just thinking of it.

He was ready for step two: research.

But where to start?

He carefully set up his makeshift laboratory on his desk, unpacking and arranging each of Dr. Finkelstein's borrowed pieces of equipment. Once satisfied with their placement, he went around his room gathering supplies he had pilfered from his visit to Christmas Town: holly sprigs, a snow globe, bows.

With a pair of tweezers, he carefully extracted a holly berry from the sprig and placed it on the microscope's slide, then twisted the machine's knob to inspect the berry more closely. He was anxious to move on to step three: hypothesis, and then step four: experimentation, so he could reach step five: observation. In his rush, he lowered the microscope lens too far, and it smashed into the slide. The glass cracked, and the berry leaked bloodred juice.

He grimaced.

Well, back to step one. And this time, less rushed.

For his next experiment, Jack connected cables between a high-voltage battery and a beaker, and he was delighted when the connection shot out sparks. Using tongs, he inserted a red-and-white-striped candy cane into the boiling burner of chemicals. But when he extracted it, he discovered that the candy had lost its red coloring and gone as limp as a comatose slug.

This isn't working at all.

Luckily, Jack wasn't the kind of skeleton to get discouraged easily. If science wasn't providing results, maybe mathematics would.

With one of the library books propped open on a book stand on his desk, he studied the geometric diagrams of a snowflake and, using scissors and paper, attempted to re-create the flake's precise crystalline symmetry. But when he unfolded the paper, the outline of a spider looked back at him instead. It was starting to seem that whatever he did, he couldn't shake the Halloween spirit that haunted his every move.

Undaunted, he skipped to step three, hypothesis, and formed a theory as he examined the black button eyes of a teddy bear. "The eyes are the window to your soul" was one of his favorite Shakespearean passages. Time to test the old bard's logic! Was the Christmas spirit hiding behind the bear's eyes? Or perhaps in its belly? With a scalpel, he performed a tidy surgery on the bear, but its stuffing revealed no answers, not even when examined beneath a magnifying glass.

Growing frustrated, Jack unhooked a decorative ball from his tree and smashed it into a glittery dust, which he poured into a boiling vat over a burner. The bubbling liquid erupted in a dazzling green glow.

Ah! At last, results!

"Interesting reaction!" He tapped his finger against his jawbone. "But what does it mean?"

Step six, conclusion, still eluded him.

But he hadn't become the Pumpkin King by giving up.

Across town, Sally gazed out the barred windows of her cell at the odd greenish light that flickered in the turret windows of Jack's house. It was well past midnight, but Jack showed no signs of turning in for the night. She thought back to the conversation she'd overheard earlier that day about a series of experiments Jack intended to conduct. That was the Pumpkin King she knew: when Jack set his skull to something, he saw it through to the end—even if it meant forgoing sleep and nourishment.

Even the Pumpkin King needs help every now and then.

She hummed to herself as she packed a basket with provisions she'd prepared during her confinement: a bottle of absinthe fortified with stinging nettle, a moldy hunk of cheese, and fish bones. She attached a thread from her sewing machine to the basket, unlocked the barred window and swung it out, and then used the machine's crank to lower the items to the ground.

She gazed once more at Jack's turret windows. The lights continued to pulse and glow.

Poor Jack. He's getting so obsessed with this Christmas thing.

The distance to the ground was dizzying. But if she waited too long, she might lose her nerve. Dr. Finkelstein had vowed never to let her out of the cell, so there was no hope of tricking him with nightshade-laced soup again. There was only one way to be free: jump.

She took a deep breath before tossing herself out the open window. She gasped as the ground rose to meet her all too fast. She collided with the dirt with a soft thud. The impact snapped the stitches that held her limbs to her body. Her legs and one of her arms ripped off and landed a few feet away.

An owl hooted overhead, and a trio of bats flew by, and not far away the Undead Ensemble played their gloomy ballads.

Sally snapped her eyes open.

She blinked.

Alive!

With a pleased smile, she sat up and used her one good arm to fish out the needle she'd tucked behind her ear. She threaded it with string from her pocket and hummed to herself as she dragged over her detached legs. She took care to add extra leaves to replace some lost stuffing as she stitched her legs and arm back on. Then she repaired her mangled hand and, at long last, tucked the needle back behind her ear and tested out her repaired body.

Good as new!

Gazing up at Jack's turret, she collected her basket and made her way past the Undead Ensemble, playing their moody notes down the winding path to Jack's house.

In his turret room, Jack was still frantically trying to solve the mystery of Christmas. He had covered every inch of his blackboard with mathematical figures and equations. Did the roasting temperature of chestnuts over an open fire equal the melting point of a snowman? What was the hypotenuse of December 25? If the sugar plum fairy left town A at a rate of one mile per hour and Sandy Claws' sleigh left town B at two miles per hour, would they collide into stardust?

He was scratching his skull, thinking, when he heard the squeak of the pulley outside his window. To his surprise, the rope was moving. Slowly, a picnic basket came into view and gently bumped against the window.

Curious, Jack swung open the window and peered downward. To his surprise, Sally was on the ground beneath his window, clutching the other end of the rope. He waved to her, a little puzzled by her presence. Their paths had crossed on occasion and she'd helped him with some sewing tasks here and there, but he was intrigued by what she might have brought him in the basket. He unhooked it from the pulley rope and set it on the windowsill. Pulling back the cloth napkin, he was delighted to find some provisions and a bottle. When he uncorked it, the most delicious smell emerged.

Why, how thoughtful!

Grinning, he leaned out the window to call down his thanks to Sally, but his grin faded.

She was gone.

Sally quickly scampered around the corner of Jack's house, closed his pumpkin-shaped gate, and pressed herself against the wall outside his yard. She'd always been shy around her fellow townsfolk—Jack most of all. When he had smiled down at her, her phantom heart had pounded so hard that she'd lost her nerve and run away.

At least he won't starve now. It wasn't as though his bones could get much thinner.

Sighing dreamily, she leaned against the wall outside his house. Would Jack ever know how she felt? Maybe one day she would gain the courage to tell him, but for now she was happy just circling him from afar, helping where she could, like a little fairy sent to brighten his nights.

A cluster of thistles grew just outside his house. Enjoying the cool wash of moonlight on her face and the freedom to stretch her limbs, she sank against a stone wall and picked one. She tore off the petals one at a time, singing the old children's rhyme to herself:

"He loathes me.
He loathes me not.
He loathes me.
He loathes me not . . ."

A strange tingling began to run down her cloth arms like static electricity, and before she knew it, the thistle shimmered and transformed into a miniature branching evergreen tree. She knew this feeling! *A vision.* Sally had had visions before, always beneath the moonlight. The last time one had happened, the thread of her sewing machine had appeared to turn into a hissing snake, and later that day, she'd found a sick baby cobra in the grass outside Dr. Finkelstein's castle and fed it herbs until it felt better.

Now the vision of the evergreen tree shimmered as colorful lights and shiny baubles appeared on its tiny branches. It looked just like Jack's Christmas tree! The vision of the little tree spun like a music box, and she marveled in awe. *So pretty.* But in the next instant, to her horror, the Christmas tree sparked and caught fire. Just like on Halloween when Jack had disguised himself as the scarecrow, it erupted in flames that decimated the branches and baubles until the tree was nothing more than ash in her hand.

Oh, no!

A terrible fear gathered in the pit of her stomach. She'd never had a vision like this, one that was so eerily dark and deadly. She knew in every part of her body that something bad was about to happen and it had to do with Jack's new favorite holiday.

I have to tell Jack!

In the morning, Jack paced inside his tower room after a long, sleepless night made better only by Sally's picnic basket. Using the scientific method, he examined the precariously balanced castle he'd made of holiday greeting cards, the cookies he'd preserved in anatomical jars, and even a toy doll with its painted-on smile mocking him. Frustrated, he hurled the doll across the room, where it landed near Zero with a soft thud and woke up the dog.

I've read every Christmas book, Jack thought with increasing agitation. *I've memorized the lyrics to every carol. And yet it eludes me!*

He collapsed in a fit of despair amid the scattered library books. He had never been known to give up. Even the previous Halloween, when the vampires had contracted the plague, and the Creature Under the Bed had decided he was afraid of the dark, and the elder witch's broomstick had snapped in two just as she'd been casting a spell on a terrified toddler, he'd improvised. He'd swept in and averted a crisis every time. It had turned out to be the best Halloween of all time!

But now he didn't feel anywhere near as confident.

As Jack rubbed his temples, Zero floated up to his friend with a framed painting clutched in his jaw.

Jack took the painting and studied it carefully. It was a portrait of him posing in the pumpkin patch in front of Spiral Hill. The Undersea Gal had painted it using squid ink from her own ink sac, and he'd always been pleased with the way she captured the curvature of his skull.

Zero gave a gentle yip.

The colorful glow of the stringed lights behind him flashed on the artwork, casting it in shades of green, then red. As red light bathed the black-and-white drawing, Jack thought for a brief flash that he was actually looking at himself wearing Sandy Claws' red suit.

"Hmm . . ." The inkling of an idea built in the back of his skull.

What if Christmas isn't as complicated as I think? he wondered. He'd spent days trying to understand the holiday when perhaps instead he should have been trying to *improve* it.

Now it all made sense. That old ghoul Sandy Claws had been hoarding Christmas all for himself! Sure, he'd done a fine job up until now—twinkling lights and flying reindeer and wrapped presents were a stroke of genius—but the man was getting old. He was probably losing his touch. If Sandy wanted his holiday to go from so-so to devilishly brilliant, then he needed help.

And who said Christmas was Sandy Claws' holiday, anyway? Why couldn't it be a holiday for everyone?

In fact, Jack thought as he stroked his chin, *I already have some ideas for improving it while giving the old man a much-deserved break at the same time . . .*

In a stroke of inspiration, he pulled the string of lights off his wan Christmas tree and dashed across his turret room, then dropped to his knees and slid over the floor toward his electric chair, where he draped the string of lights over the chair's back and plugged it in.

He cackled in delight as the lights flashed and crackled. Gone was their humdrum holiday glow . . . Now the lights sparked! They threatened to explode!

Now *that* was magic!

Jack decided that Christmas needed a strong shock to bring it back to life, and he was just the skeleton to flip the switch.

"He-he-he!"

Outside, just beyond the wall surrounding Jack's house, Sally slumbered in the patch where she had found the thistles and had her terrifying vision. She awoke to the crowing of the reanimated corpse of a rooster and was surprised to find she wasn't alone.

Several townspeople had gathered at Jack's gate, frowning up at the turret. Like Sally, they had also noticed Jack's odd, obsessive behavior.

The vampire brothers lifted their cloaks against the rising sun.

"Something's up with Jack," they cautioned, peering up at his spindly house before they swept away to the safety of the shadows. The Wolfman passed by next, growling worriedly before shaking his head and stalking away.

As Sally brushed the dirt off her dress, the Corpse Kid huffed past, tugging his mother by his leash.

"Something's up with Jack," he echoed. Everyone in town seemed to have noticed Jack's spiraling obsession, but no one knew what to do about it.

Sally listened to their fears, which weren't so different from her own. She was in the midst of debating what to do when Jack threw open his windows and thrust his head out.

"Eureka!" he cried in triumph.

Sally and the rest of the townspeople loitering around Jack's gates looked up in surprise.

Jack leaned out his window like a king presiding over his kingdom. He raised his hand in the air as strings of colorful lights blinked behind him. "This year, Christmas will be ours!"

The townsfolk all cheered at the Pumpkin King's proclamation . . . except for Sally, who hugged the bars of Jack's gate, fearful of her vision.

CHAPTER ELEVEN

301 DAYS TILL HALLOWEEN

A LINE OF MONSTERS wound through town, starting at the steps to Town Hall and stretching all the way to the cemetery. A hum of excitement was in the air. This Christmas thing had to be particularly terrifying if Jack was so enthusiastic about it. The monsters whispered to one another, trying to guess what role each one of them would be assigned to play in the yuletide horrors.

"Patience, everyone," the Mayor announced

through his megaphone. "Jack has a special job for each of you."

Standing in line behind the saxophone player from the Undead Ensemble, Sally anxiously rested her chin on one palm. She had overheard the excited chatter from the others but couldn't join in their enthusiasm. The thistles' frightening vision was too fresh.

What did it mean?

Tragedy, a voice warned in the back of her mind.

The Mayor called through his megaphone, "Dr. Finkelstein? Your Christmas assignment is ready."

At the mention of the doctor's name, Sally gasped and looked around the crowd. Dr. Finkelstein was there? The Mayor had summoned everyone in Halloween Town to meet at the auditorium, but Dr. Finkelstein was often exempt from such gatherings, left to toil on his important experiments in the laboratory. But now she heard the drone of his wheelchair somewhere nearby.

I have to hide! she thought. Her scalp still ached from when that limping hunchback, Igor, dragged her back by the hair last time she had escaped.

She started to move to the back of the line, but the hulking blue-skinned Behemoth was right behind her, blocking the path to the cemetery. Instead she darted to the far side of the wishing well, where a gibbet rattled in the wind over the brackish water.

She ducked behind the fountain, knitting her hands together anxiously.

Dr. Finkelstein wheeled into her sight. He stopped just a few feet from where she had been standing in line and snaked his head around, searching the crowd.

He's looking for me.

But to her relief, Behemoth was too dull-witted to realize who the doctor was searching for, and the saxophone player wasn't the type to rat anyone out.

"Dr. Finkelstein, to the front of the line," the Mayor said, beckoning to him. Frustrated by not having found Sally, the doctor grumbled as he steered his wheelchair toward Town Hall. The night before, he had gone to release her from her cell. *You can come out now,* he'd said, *if you promise to behave.*

But he'd only found an empty cell. She'd escaped—*again.*

Inside the auditorium, Jack was onstage, busy doling out responsibilities to Halloween Town's residents, while the Mayor perched on a dangerously tall stool and marked off names on his roster. The vampires were waiting eagerly for their assignment. Jack dug through his Christmas trunk full of toys until he found a baby doll with pink cheeks and a darling blue swaddle who let out a sweet mechanical "waaa" when tipped upright.

"What kind of noise is that for a baby to make?" the head vampire demanded, recoiling from the doll. The other vampires lifted their cloaks over their faces to ward off the gentle coos.

"Perhaps it can be improved?" Jack suggested.

The most optimistic of the vampires thrust his finger in the air. "No problem!"

Delighted, Jack clapped his hands. "I knew it."

As the vampires glided away under the protection of their umbrellas, Dr. Finkelstein wheeled across the auditorium stage.

Jack pressed his hands together in delight. "Doctor, thank you for coming." He moved aside some presents in the trunk until he found the book he was looking for, titled *Santa's Workshop*. He opened it to a page he had bookmarked that showed a silhouette of Sandy Claws' fierce flying reindeer.

"We need some of these." He tapped the picture.

Jack knew that building flying reindeer was no easy feat, but he felt confident that if anyone could achieve it, it was Halloween Town's resident evil scientist. He'd considered asking the witches if they could summon straw reindeer dummies to life but then decided that simply wouldn't do. Reindeer were *essential* to Christmas' success.

They needed to be real flesh and bone—or at least bone. Dr. Finkelstein had reanimated so many stitched-together bodies that Jack didn't trust anyone else with the task. Just look at what beautiful work the doctor had done making Sally.

"Hmm," Dr. Finkelstein said, squinting at the illustrations through his dark glasses. He nodded to himself as he considered the reindeer's nimble legs and sharp antlers. "Their construction should be exceedingly simple, I think."

The Mayor, tottering up high on his stool next to the podium, checked Dr. Finkelstein's name off the list and jotted down his task. "How horrible our Christmas will be," he said in delight with the happier of his two faces.

"No," Jack corrected him patiently, which prompted the Mayor to quickly change to his worried face. "How *jolly*."

"Oh." The Mayor grimaced. As much as he trusted Jack, this Christmas thing was still a bit of a head-scratcher. He pressed a worried hand against his face, leaving a smear of black ink on his cheek. "How *jolly* our Christmas will be."

The Mayor wondered if he would ever get it right.

A bone flew out of nowhere and smacked the Mayor in the nose. A baseball followed, and another small round object, and he growled like a bulldog chasing a bee. He finally caught sight of his attackers.

Three snickering children wearing Halloween masks came out from wherever they had been hiding.

Oogie Boogie's gang!

The Mayor recoiled before asking, "What are *you* doing here?"

A little boy in a devil costume cackled and said, "Jack sent for us . . ."

". . . specifically . . ." added a blue-haired girl dressed as a witch.

". . . by name," finished a stout boy in a skeleton mask.

Taunting the Mayor, the three of them brandished slingshots made out of wishbones.

"Lock," the devil said, introducing himself as he took off his red mask to show his real face.

"Shock!" the girl said, giggling sweetly as she removed her own mask.

"And Barrel!" chimed in the shortest one, taking off his mask to give his lollipop a lick.

The Mayor pointed his megaphone in Jack's direction and called in an urgent whisper to him, reminding him that these were Oogie Boogie's helpers. He grimaced so hard that his teeth chattered.

"Ah!" Jack knelt on one knee to be face to face with the mischievous trio. "Halloween's finest trick-or-treaters." He swept his arms out and herded them close as he lowered his voice. "The job I have for you is top secret." He smashed a bony fist into his other hand to emphasize its importance. "It requires craft"—he waggled his fingers in the air—"cunning"—and curled his bony fingers into a claw—"and mischief."

The three of them beamed behind their masks.

"And we thought you didn't like us, Jack," Shock purred. Lock and Barrel started snickering, elbowing each other in the ribs.

Jack wagged a hard finger at them. "Absolutely no one is to know about it. Not. A. Soul." He gave them a stern look from his dark eye sockets. "Now . . ."

He bent close and whispered his plans into their little ears.

The Mayor pressed his megaphone against his own ear, straining to hear what Jack was saying. But it was no good. Jack's voice was too muffled. The Mayor held up the megaphone, peering into it to see if it was clogged. *Ah!* It was. If he could just fish out the obstruction . . .

"Eee!" the spider from his collar bit on to his finger, and he let out a shriek.

Escaped again, eh? The little eight-legged scamp . . .

He squished the spider back onto his shirt collar, where it belonged, giving it a firm look of disapproval. He hadn't hired the spider to be his necktie only for it to keep wandering off.

"And one more thing." Jack's voice took on an edge as he snatched Lock, who was trying to sneak off, by his devil tail. He picked up the boy under the arms, giving him a good solid shake. "Leave that no-account Oogie Boogie out of this!"

It was a risk to trust Oogie Boogie's gang. Lock, Shock, and Barrel were as thick as thieves with that squirming sack of trouble. Halloween Town's foulest resident mostly stayed underground these days, scheming in his lair outside town. But Jack hadn't forgotten his history with Oogie Boogie. There had been a time before he was the Pumpkin King when Halloween Town was almost ruled by a Bug King instead . . .

But Oogie Boogie's reign had never come to be.

"Whatever you say, Jack." Barrel swayed back and forth sweetly, clutching his lollipop.

"Of course, Jack." Shock pressed a hand to her chest as a promise.

"Wouldn't dream of it, Jack." Lock bowed but started snickering mischievously halfway through, setting off the rest of the trio, who giggled and cackled.

Behind their backs, where neither Jack nor the Mayor could see, all three of them had their fingers crossed.

As soon as they were dismissed, Lock, Shock, and Barrel traipsed from Town Hall through the town gates to the festering pit they called home. Ever since Oogie Boogie's attempt to rule town as the Bug King had failed, he had taken up residence in the wastelands. Since he was persona non grata in town, he'd decided to create his own kingdom of worms.

Not even the mischievous trick-or-treaters could stomach Oogie Boogie's dank, wriggling den, so instead they lived in a tree house right over it, built in the burned-out remains of what had once been the largest tree in the area, before

Oogie Boogie had burned that whole part of the forest down.

They dashed across a swinging bridge to the base of their tree house, where they tumbled into a hanging cage that served as an elevator between their tree house and Oogie Boogie's lair.

They pulled off their masks.

"Kidnap the Sandy Claws!" Shock said, rattling the cage's bars. "This is big, boys. Real big!"

"We could draw straws to see who gets to do it," Barrel offered, holding up three thin bones of various lengths.

"No way, this will take all three of us!" Shock threw the lever that raised the cage into their tree house of horrors. Once it stopped, they tumbled out into their home. "I know!" she said. "We'll set a trap. Put in bait he can't resist. And then . . . *bam*! We trap the fat man."

Barrel scampered across the living room and grabbed a mousetrap. He placed his lollipop inside the trap to illustrate her point. A shiny beetle trotted into the trap, and Shock closed the cage door behind it. Barrel snatched up the trapped bug with a cruel gleam in his eye.

"I have a better idea!" Lock said, jumping on the table they used as a kitchen counter. He filled a pot to the brim and then set it on the oven to boil. "We'll push that juicy red lobster-man into a giant pot and watch him boil alive!"

Barrel tossed the bug in the mousetrap to him. Lock caught it and doused the poor bug in the boiling vat while licking his lips. "Ooh, he'd taste good with some butter!" After a minute, Lock fished out the caged bug, which had turned green and sickly.

He tossed the cage to Shock.

Clutching the poor caged bug, Shock twirled over to the wall of their tree house that was covered with various Halloween masks hanging on nails. In the center of the wall, a chute opened. It snaked down from the tree house into Oogie Boogie's deep pit below.

Shock hurled the caged bug down the chute, and the other two bowed.

They listened to the *clank-clank-clank* as the cage tumbled down the long chute. Then they began to giggle along to the clanking sounds.

Lock eyed a cannon and fireworks in the corner of the room and suggested, "Why don't we just blow Sandy Claws up?"

Shock smacked him in the head. "You dolt. You're no better than the worms. If we bring Mr. Sandy Claws to Jack in pieces, what do you think Jack will do to us? Beat us to a pulp!"

Once the offering to Oogie Boogie was finished, Shock dragged her coconspirators into a dirty bathroom, where she pushed them into a rusted-out claw-foot tub. "Oogie Boogie is going to be so pleased! This is just what he's been waiting for. His chance to work his way back into town. To take over again, this time for good! And then he'll reward *us*!"

Barrel tugged on the tub drain's chain, and the tub shook itself awake, stretched out its claws, and then obediently padded in the direction Barrel urged it.

Shock jumped out of the tub and pulled back the curtain that served as a door to their closet, then took a black box from within. "Okay, listen. Here's what we'll do. Sandy Claws likes presents, right? Well, we'll give him a present. A *big* present. A present just bursting with *surprise*. When he opens the box, we three will be there to snatch him!" She opened the box to demonstrate, but before she could slam it closed, three scorpions jumped out onto Barrel.

Barrel just giggled. "Bye-bye, Mr. Sandy Claws."

The three of them began to fill the bathtub with fireworks, animal traps, and sharpened spears. As the coldhearted trick-or-treaters continued to plan their Sandy Claws trap, the caged bug Shock had stuffed down the chute finally tumbled out the other end. It landed on a dark circular table in the middle of a massive cave.

A hulking shadow fell over the sickly little bug, which let out a plaintive squeak.

The shadow gave a deep, rumbling *he-he-he*. Oogie Boogie had listened to his minions describing their dastardly plans overhead, and he liked what he'd heard.

"Sandy Claws, huh?" he mused, and, with a giant slurp, sucked the little bug right out of the cage and into the dark abyss of his mouth.

After his meal, he tossed a pair of red dice and laughed as a snake slithered through the dice's skeleton eyeholes.

CHAPTER TWELVE

298 DAYS TILL HALLOWEEN

"IT GOES something like this." Jack held up a sleigh bell strap and tapped out a tinkling song on the bells one by one. The bright notes danced toward the ears of the Undead Ensemble. "How about it?" Jack asked. "Think you can manage?" He'd spent the past few grueling days doling out assignments to Halloween Town's residents, and with the Mayor's help, they were nearly at the end of the list.

The sax player chuckled to himself. The ensemble could manage, all right. They'd been playing together since their deaths nearly a hundred years earlier and knew the entire funeral catalog by heart. They'd never played a cheerful ditty like this, but with a few modifications, it could be a halfway decent jam.

The tiny man who lived inside the bass and served as the band's conductor announced, "A one, and a two, and a three, and a . . ."

The musicians threw themselves into the song. The dirge groaned to life with flat notes and dismal rhythm. Towering over them on his tall stool, the Mayor nodded in approval and called, "Next!"

"Fantastic," Jack said to the musicians. He could feel the melody singing in his bones, though it didn't have quite the same joyfulness as his version. Well, they'd master it eventually. He draped the sleigh bell strap over the colossal accordion player's neck. "Now, why don't you all practice on that and we'll be in great shape."

As the musicians shuffled off to the tinkling sound of the sleigh bells, Sally stepped onto the stage. She was wringing her hands together in worry.

Finally, a chance to tell him about my vision, she thought.

Jack's hollow eyes softened when he saw her. She'd been so kind to send up refreshments in the picnic basket, yet she'd disappeared before he could thank her. Besides, Sally's Christmas job was the most important of all, even more so than Dr. Finkelstein's mission to create flying reindeer. In a way, all of Jack's Christmas success or failure rested on her capable shoulders.

"Sally." He brushed his bony fingers against her elbow, guiding her farther along on the stage. "I need your help more than anyone."

"You certainly do, Jack." She wrung her hands harder. "I had the most terrible vision."

Nodding along, Jack dug through his trunk of objects from Christmas Town, tossing aside a gingerbread man. "That's splendid."

"No!" Sally sighed. Jack wasn't listening to her. "It was about your Christmas." Sally moved toward him, wishing she could grab him and shake some sense into him. "There was smoke . . ." She looked to the floor as she remembered the terrifying premonition and then threw her hands up in the air. "And fire!"

Jack chuckled as he gave Sally a reassuring smile. "That's not *my* Christmas. My Christmas is filled with laughter and joy." He waved a candy cane in the air for emphasis, then dropped it back into the trunk and picked up a framed piece of art. "Ah! And this."

He held out the artwork for Sally to see. It was the portrait of him posing in the pumpkin patch in front of Spiral Hill.

He flipped over a taped-on piece of wax paper on which he'd traced his outline and added a handsome red suit.

"My Sandy Claws outfit." He thrust a long finger toward Sally. "I want you to make it."

Sally barely glanced at the drawing. Pressing her hands to her chest, she insisted, "Jack, please listen to me. It's going to be a disaster."

"How could it be? Just follow the pattern." He felt certain that Sally was only nervous about the task at hand, so he helpfully pointed out the details on the drawing. "This part's red. The trim is white—"

"It's a mistake, Jack." The urgency in Sally's voice didn't give Jack pause. What was she worried about? She was an excellent seamstress! She'd even had the brilliant idea to add white pinstripes to his Halloween suit after bats kept flying into him, unable to tell his clothes apart from the black of night.

"Now don't be modest. Who else is clever enough to make my Sandy Claws outfit?"

Sally let out a frustrated sigh. He still wasn't listening to her. This Christmas obsession of his was blinding him to what was right in front of him.

"Next!" the Mayor called through his megaphone.

Jack pressed a hand against the small of Sally's back and guided her toward the stage's wings. "I have every confidence in you."

He whirled around to address Behemoth, who had just wheezed his way up to the stage and was ogling the trunkful of toys with his unblinking round eyes.

Sally sighed to herself and shook her head. "But it seems wrong to me. Very wrong."

As Sally disappeared into the shadows, Jack presented Behemoth with a small wooden doll. "This device is called a nutcracker," he said, moving a lever that made the doll's wooden jaw clack open and closed.

Behemoth moaned in excitement and reached for the doll, but before he could grasp it, the auditorium's door flew open dramatically.

"Jack! Jack! We got him!"

It was Lock, Shock, and Barrel. The three children practically danced down the aisle in their excitement. Their walking claw-foot tub trotted along steadily behind them, carrying a large black bag tied up with twine.

"We got him!" they cried again in unison.

"Perfect!" Jack clapped his hands as he rushed down from the stage to meet them. "Open it up. Quickly!"

He'd rehearsed a short speech he was going to recite to Sandy Claws. It was quite an honor to meet another king of a holiday town, and he wanted to make the best first impression on such an important figure.

Barrel climbed onto the edge of the tub and tugged at the twine until the knot came untied, which sent him tumbling backward with a cry.

A giant pink blur sprang out of the bag, surprising Lock and Shock enough that they shrieked and jumped backward. The air filled with the smell of fresh-cut grass and caramel eggs. The pink blur landed in the aisle and lifted its cute black nose to the air, sniffing. It had long fluffy ears and marshmallowy fur and was holding a sunny yellow basket filled with wrapped chocolate eggs.

"That's not Sandy Claws!" Jack yelled.

"It isn't?" Shock said.

"Who is it?" Lock asked.

The pink creature bounded on powerful rear legs down the aisle, its curious nose inspecting everything, until it hopped onstage and gave Behemoth a wary look.

Behemoth yelled happily as he lurched toward it. "*Bunny!*"

Faced with a looming undead plumber impaled by an ax, the terrified rabbit scrambled off the stage, squeaking in horror, and dove straight back into the black bag, where it shivered in fright.

"*Not* Sandy Claws," Jack snapped. That was what he got for trusting Oogie Boogie's gang! If he didn't know better, he'd think the rabble-rousers had nabbed the wrong holiday king on purpose. "Take him back."

"We followed your instructions," Lock insisted.

"We went through the door," Barrel added.

Jack towered over them with a scowl splitting his skull. "*Which* door? There's more than one!" He jabbed a finger in the air. "Sandy Claws is behind the door shaped like this." From his suit's inside pocket he took a tree-shaped cookie slathered in green icing and dangled it before them.

Shock threw her hands around Lock's neck. "I told you!" As Lock gagged for air, Barrel slapped Shock across the cheek, and she spun around, then tripped and fell backward. They all tangled together in a scrabble.

"Knock it off!" Jack said.

He massaged his aching skull. Could those three get anything right? If they botched another attempt, he'd have to do the job himself, and he couldn't afford to take the time away from his Christmas preparations.

Barrel kicked Shock in the ribs. "Ow! Ow!"

That's it. Jack hooked his fingers into the sides of his mouth and pulled back his skull as he posed with one of his most terrifying faces.

"Rrrraaarrrrr!"

His roar shook the entire Town Hall auditorium. The trick-or-treaters forgot about their disagreement and jumped to their feet. Lock and Barrel cowered behind Shock, shivering. Three identical shrieks slipped from their throats.

Satisfied, Jack turned to the giant pink bunny quivering in the bathtub. "I'm very sorry for the inconvenience, sir."

As the bathtub began to trot off to carry the bunny back to the Hinterlands, Jack turned on the trick-or-treaters with a snarl. "Take *him* home first. And apologize again!"

The trio shuffled behind the claw-foot tub obediently, not wanting to see another of Jack's frightful faces.

"Be careful with Sandy Claws when you fetch him," Jack called after them. "Treat him nicely."

"Got it," Lock called over his shoulder.

"We'll get it right next time!" all three chimed in.

Jack shook his skull wearily. Halloween Town's most mischievous trick-or-treaters might not be the best ambassadors to send to a fellow holiday land, but he didn't know anyone else with enough tricks up their sleeves to get the job done.

He hoped next time they didn't come back with an oversized turkey.

Lightning crashed outside Dr. Finkelstein's castle as he toiled late into the night. A headless human corpse lay strapped to his operating table. He'd selected the finest specimens of various body parts and stitched them together with sturdy wire that wouldn't unravel with a simple tug, as Sally's had.

All that was left was to select the perfect head.

"You will be a decided improvement over that treacherous Sally," he muttered to the corpse as he pressed a button to rotate the machine that held different skull possibilities. Did he want one with freakishly wide cheekbones? Or a chin curved like a hook? Or perhaps one with glistening fangs? That could come in handy for opening tin cans.

"Master . . ." A somber voice oozed its way up the spiral ramp. Dr. Finkelstein set down the machine's controls and wheeled to his desk as his assistant, Igor, limped into the laboratory, carrying rolls of paper. Igor's hunchback cast long shadows over the cold metal desk. His one good eye sparkled with delight: the doctor would be pleased with what he'd located.

"The plans," Igor moaned as he unrolled blueprints next to a selection of curving bones he'd pillaged from the animal cemetery.

"Excellent, Igor." The doctor tossed his hunchbacked assistant a dog biscuit as a reward before examining the diagrams.

So Jack wants flying reindeer, he thought. *Very well. I'll make the fiercest beasts ever to stalk the stars.*

CHAPTER THIRTEEN

35 DAYS TILL ~~HALLOWEEN~~ CHRISTMAS

THE CLOCK in Town Hall's tower counted off the twelve months of the year instead of twelve hours in a day. For a year now, the residents of Halloween Town had watched the clock's batwing hands sweep in a steady circle as days came and went in a flurry of garland stringing and present wrapping. The clock's hands passed October 31 with no scares, no dancing scarecrows, no nightmares. For the first time, Halloween Town had no Halloween.

The town barely noticed. Jack's yuletide

excitement was as infectious as smallpox, spreading through the ghoulish population until each undead soul rose early to toil on their Christmas tasks and went to bed grinning because December 25 was one day closer.

When only a few weeks remained before the holiday, the vampires pointed out that the DAYS TO HALLOWEEN countdown sign, which had hung above the clock for as long as anyone could remember, was no longer applicable. So the Undersea Gal and Behemoth dragged out a ladder and rigged up a new sign to cover the old one.

DAYS TO XMAS the new sign read in Behemoth's childlike handwriting.

Everyone agreed it was a vast improvement.

The monsters' excited chatter filled the air as the Devil untangled strings of sinister red lights that looked like glowing eyes, while the vampires braved the sunlight beneath umbrellas to deliver cans of paint to the toy makers, who were busy constructing roadkill teddy bears and possessed dolls with midnight-black hair. The Clown with the Tear-Away Face packed Pandora's boxes with cute little curses that would haunt the children on Christmas morning.

"Making Christmas!" they exclaimed as they watched the clock's arms move closer to the big date each day.

Sally listened to the sounds of the monsters' hard work from behind the heavy drapes of her makeshift sewing workshop. Once Dr. Finkelstein had sworn that he was well and truly done with her and that she was on her own, she'd set to work on Jack's new costume.

As the merriment grew more raucous outside, Sally leaned over her sewing machine, her brow wrinkled in concentration as she ran thread through the red velvet fabric Jack had asked her to use. The drawing of Jack in his Sandy Claws suit hung on the wall behind her sewing table. She told herself it was for reference as she made the suit, but she caught herself staring at it several times a day with a furrowed brow, remembering her vision.

Oh, Jack. I wish you'd listened to me.

But months had passed and her vision hadn't come true, and she'd found herself swept up in the same infectious excitement as the rest of the town. It was only whenever she caught sight of the drawing of Jack that she remembered her terrible premonition.

He was the Pumpkin King, not Sandy Claws. Why was he trying to be something he wasn't? Was this entire Christmas holiday a terrible mistake?

Worries stitched a line through her thoughts as she cut the next segment from her pattern. The chatter grew louder outside her workshop, and she peered out, curious. Jack had arrived in the Town Square to inspect everyone's work. The Corpse Kid and Mummy Boy proudly pounded toy cars to smithereens, beaming at him.

"The children will be so surprised when they open these presents!" the Corpse Kid giggled.

Jack patted the Corpse Kid on the back. "Indeed they will. This year, Christmas is ours!"

Everyone cheered. They were determined to do Christmas *right*. Who wouldn't want a delightful vampire teddy bear or a game of checkers with scorpions and beetles? Their unique toys and gifts would bring such delight to little boys and girls everywhere!

Ghosts carrying poison-laced paints floated up from the wishing well. They passed by the Undead Ensemble's accordion player, who pushed a wheelbarrow filled with jack-o'-lanterns that would soon be turned into orange-faced baby dolls. Rats scuttled over the ground with ribbons between their teeth.

High up in the castle overlooking the Town Square, Dr. Finkelstein and Igor flipped the electrical switch to bring the reindeer corpses to life. As electricity snapped in the air, the doctor raised his small fists in triumph. His excitement got the best of him, and he toppled over onto his desk, knocking into an extra skull Igor had found in the cemetery. He picked it up, marveling at the elegant curvature of the bone.

Hmm, he thought. *A beautiful skull . . . for a beautiful lady?*

Back in the center of town, the Mayor drove Jack's snowmobile, carrying their top secret Christmas plans in the attached wagon, while townspeople carried out long wooden tables. When lined up just right, the tables not only served as extra work space but also made an elevated ramp. The Corpse Kid and Mummy Boy managed to hop into the snowmobile when the Mayor's back was turned, and tested out the ramp, knocking the tottering Mayor right off the platform to the ground. He dusted off his hat and kept grinning.

"They'll talk about this for years, Jack," the witches purred.

A vampire showed off a present wrapped with a grinning snake. "Did you know a snake makes an excellent bow?" The other vampires were deep in concentration painting bullet holes onto a possessed windup duck. They had spent days selecting the perfect shade of red: they were experts in blood, after all.

"Look what I made from a dead rat!" The Harlequin Demon shoved a smashed rat carcass he had fashioned into a cap onto the head of the Undead Ensemble's saxophone player, who had reluctantly agreed to be his model. The demon stuck a feather in the hat for an added flourish.

The sax player shook his head, regretting his role.

Jack tapped a bony finger against his chin as he inspected the Harlequin Demon's handiwork. "Hmm, an excellent hat, but perhaps try something less . . . deceased? How about a bat?"

The Harlequin Demon set to work while the sax player rolled his eyes.

Jack rubbed his hands together as he moved to the next workstation, where the Melting Man was about to wrap up a dead turtle he'd run over with the Mayor's hearse. Jack took the turtle and gave it a shake; the head fell off.

"Try again!" Jack patted the Melting Man's bald head, but his hand stuck and took several tugs to get free.

Jack nodded to himself while he watched Dr. Hyde and his demonic miniature alter egos, each one half the size of the next largest, stacking nesting dolls that echoed their diminishing sizes.

My dream is coming true, Jack mused. *It's really happening . . . even if it's not* exactly *as I envisioned.*

The townspeople had come a long way toward embracing the magical Christmas spirit he'd felt when he'd visited Sandy Claws' town, but they still needed a little more guidance. Jack reminded himself to be patient with them. They'd never seen a sleigh full of presents. They hadn't seen the elves' jolly toy factory. Besides, a snake tied up in a bow seemed perfectly lovely to him. It was much more exciting than a lifeless ribbon; that was for sure.

The clock ticked down another day, and the monsters cheered.

"Just a few more days!" the Wolfman howled.

CHAPTER FOURTEEN

2 DAYS TILL ~~HALLOWEEN~~ CHRISTMAS

IN A FARAWAY land, a different song rode on the wind.

"Making Christmas!" the Christmas Town elves exclaimed, but instead of talking about snakes and slime, they discussed sugar and spice.

Above the elves' toy factory, a clock also ticked down the days until December 25. The elves worked round the clock, barely stopping for hot cocoa and cookies to meet the holiday deadline.

An assembly line cheerfully produced rocking horses painted red and green; not a single one was known to bite. On the opposite side of the factory, the elf seamstresses pedaled oversized sewing machines to make teddy bears that gave hugs, not smallpox. And in the bakery, fleets of bakers mixed sugar and flour for gingerbread men; not an ounce of poison was added.

On the hill overlooking Christmas Town, three mischievous trick-or-treaters watched the elves' preparations in disgust.

Lock, Shock, Barrel, and their walking bathtub had squeezed through the carved wooden door built into a Hinterlands tree and tumbled down a swirling vortex of frosty air to find themselves on a snowy hill overlooking a village that twinkled with holiday lights.

They had found the right door at last.

Christmas Town.

Lock started down the mountain. Shock tripped him just to be nasty. He kicked her in return, and the three of them and the bathtub slid down the hill until they landed with a thud in front of the biggest house in town, with fir-scented smoke puffing out of the chimney and warm candlelight in the windows.

They'd never seen anything like this magical land. Over the past few months they had explored every other world through the mystical doorways in the Hinterlands trees. After they'd returned the Easter Bunny to his springtime meadow, they'd frightened baby chicks and smashed decorated eggs. They'd instigated a food fight in Thanksgiving Town, drenching one another with gravy and mashed potatoes. Each world was so wonderfully new and wonderfully easy to terrorize. It had been like taking Halloween candy from a baby. But Christmas Town . . . *this* was something truly special.

Oogie Boogie's gang tiptoed over to peek in the toy factory windows, where they spied on the elves packaging up teddy bears. They sneered. Back in Halloween Town, their friends were doing a much better job stuffing boxes with creepy-crawly toys.

Christmas Town's elves fed and groomed eight robust reindeer, but Lock, Shock, and Barrel all agreed that Dr. Finkelstein's skeleton animals were far superior. They didn't need to be fed at all.

The hands on the clock above the toy factory were dangerously close to December 25. Only two days left until Christmas! *Enough dillydallying*, the trick-or-treaters decided. They'd had their fun wreaking havoc on the other holiday towns; now it was time to capture Sandy Claws—or face Jack's wrath.

Shock hissed for the boys to be quiet while she peeked into the windows of each cottage. Sleeping children. Elves decorating trees. *Ah!* At last, she found the right house. Inside, a large man in a red suit was reading aloud a list of children's names to his wife, who helped him decide who had been naughty and who had been nice.

It was really him.

The legend.

The *terror*.

Sandy Claws.

Shock elbowed her coconspirators to signal for them to put on their masks. Once they were fully in costume, they each clutched a side of their giant black plastic treat bag and snickered to themselves.

Shock rang the doorbell. It chimed with a festive melody. In the next moment, the door swung open and they were looking straight into the rosy-cheeked face of that old devil Sandy Claws.

"Trick or treat!" Lock, Shock, and Barrel sang in unison.

Sandy Claws' woolly white eyebrows knit together as he leaned down for a closer look at the unfamiliar children. He was quite sure none of these were on the list of nice boys and girls he'd been going over with Mrs. Claws.

"Hmm?" he asked, perplexed.

Now!

The trick-or-treaters leapt up to throw the bag around Sandy Claws, making quick work of wrestling the confused king of Christmas Town into their walking bathtub.

As they rode on top of the bag struggling in the bathtub, Shock giggled to herself. *Naughty or nice? Definitely naughty.*

CHAPTER FIFTEEN

THE DAY BEFORE CHRISTMAS

JACK ADMIRED himself in the full-length mirror in Sally's sewing workshop. The long white beard she'd made of spider silk gave him a dashing, thoughtful air. The red suit fit his narrow bones like a glove, and the white trim at the neck and sleeves was perfect down to the last stitch.

"You don't look like yourself, Jack, not at all," Sally muttered as she sewed a bit more trim onto his sleeve.

"Isn't that wonderful?" Jack turned back to

the mirror to admire the white trim at the collar. "It couldn't be more wonderful!"

"But you're the Pumpkin King." She unhooked his portrait from the wall and pulled back the wax paper to show Jack as she knew him best: in his black striped suit with his dashing bat bow tie.

He took the portrait from her and promptly snapped it in two over his knee. He tossed the pieces to the floor dramatically. "Not anymore! And I feel so much better now."

Sally grumbled uneasily as she finished stitching his left sleeve's trim. "Jack, I know you think something's missing, but—" She was so distracted by the memory of her vision that she jabbed the needle into his finger bone.

"Ow!" On instinct, he popped the hurt finger into his mouth.

"Sorry," she offered.

Jack remembered that as a skeleton, he felt no pain, and took the finger out of his mouth.

He admired himself again in the mirror. "You're right. Something is missing, but what? I've got the beard, the coat, the boots . . ."

"Jack! Jack!"

The mirror reflected something outside the sewing workshop that stole his attention. Before Sally could stop him, he ran out into the Town Square, where monsters loaded packages into the sleigh they'd made out of a coffin and a barrel. The skeletal reindeer, draped in festive garlands, danced over the wooden boards of the elevated ramp, eager to take flight.

Lock, Shock, and Barrel paraded into the Town Square sitting atop an enormous bundle tied up in their walking bathtub.

"This time we bagged him!" the three exclaimed.

Lock jumped off the bag and skipped up to Jack. "This time we *really* did!"

"He sure is big, Jack," Barrel said, patting the sack beneath him.

"And heavy!" Shock insisted.

She and Lock pulled the rope to open the bag. Immediately, the white-bearded man in a red suit struggled free.

"Let me out!" he demanded in a huff.

Gasps filled the air as monsters eyed the fierce king of Christmas Town. The terrible Sandy Claws! In the flesh! Jack was the only one who didn't cower before him.

Jack turned on his undead charm as he approached the bearded man. "Sandy Claws, in person! What a pleasure to meet you."

He thrust out his skeletal hand and clutched Sandy Claws' black-gloved one. He gasped in astonishment as he examined the man's petite digits.

"Why, you have *hands*. You don't have claws at all!"

Sandy Claws pushed his red stocking cap back over his aching head. After he had spent so long crammed up in the black bag, it took his eyes a minute to adjust. He looked around in a daze.

What was this awful place? These monsters? This drab gray sky? These angular buildings that grinned ghoulishly like they were alive?

"Where am I?" he asked, still out of sorts.

Beaming, Jack leaned in until he was just a few inches from Sandy's face. "Surprised, aren't you?" He swept his hands back to show off his town. "I knew you would be. You don't need to have another worry about Christmas this year."

Sandy Claws still felt like he must be trapped in a nightmare. Sticky candies from those three naughty trick-or-treaters were caught in his beard, making a mess of everything.

He blinked, considering Jack's words. "What?"

Jack reassuringly rested a hand on Sandy's back. "Consider this a vacation, Sandy. A reward. It's your turn to take it easy." He plucked a candy from Sandy Claws' beard.

"But there must be some mistake," Sandy sputtered.

"See that he's comfortable," Jack commanded Lock, Shock, and Barrel.

Gleefully, the masked children pounced on Sandy and wrestled him back into the Halloween bag.

"Just a second, fellas!" Jack ordered when Sandy was halfway back in the bag. Jack leaned in close, stroking his chin and examining Sandy Claws. "Of course! That's what I'm missing!" He snatched the red cap off Sandy's head and placed it on his own. "Thanks."

Sandy protested, "But . . . You just can't . . ." His voice dimmed as the trick-or-treaters crammed him back into the bag and retied the rope. The claw-foot tub stretched its porcelain limbs, then started the long walk out of town.

"Hold on." Sandy's muffled voice came from inside the bag. "Where are we going now?"

Oogie Boogie's gang snickered as they rode atop him.

Once Sandy Claws had departed for his restful retreat, Jack stroked the hat.

"Ho, ho, ho!" he attempted in a flat voice, then shook his head. "No." It didn't sound right at all. He tried again, deeper this time. "Ho, ho, ho!"

Sally, wringing her hands, watched outside her sewing workshop. "This is much worse than I thought. Much worse." She pressed her hands to her face. Kidnapping Sandy Claws? He was in incredible danger with those naughty little children. They'd take him straight to Oogie Boogie's lair; she knew it. Why was Jack letting this happen? Didn't he know better?

This whole Christmas thing had simply gone too far.

Jack practiced a higher-pitched *ho-ho-ho*, then shook his head again. Still not perfect.

"I know!" Sally grabbed her cloth bag and ran out of the sewing workshop, then moved quietly through the streets, though everyone was too busy packing presents in the coffin sleigh to notice the rag doll making her way to Dr. Finkelstein's castle.

The castle was the single place in Halloween Town Sally dreaded most, but try as she might, she couldn't shake the terrible premonition that something awful would come from Jack's obsession with Christmas. Jack wouldn't listen to her, and the other town residents were all too dazzled by his plans to listen, either. So she simply had to take matters into her own hands.

She had learned that Dr. Finkelstein kept a key to the castle's front door hidden beneath a little stone gargoyle in the garden. For such a brilliant man, he could be surprisingly forgetful, especially when it came to trivialities like remembering to take his keys with him when he left. A cold feeling overcame her as she tiptoed along the outside of the castle. She needed to get inside to stop Jack's plan, but what if she was caught?

Would the doctor lock her in her cell again? Would he rip open her seams and scatter her stuffing in the cemetery?

Fortunately, her soft cotton boots barely made a creak as she unlocked the front door and climbed the castle's ramp.

High up on another floor, a saw whined to life. Sally relaxed. Dr. Finkelstein must be working in his laboratory. When he was up there, he tended to become so engrossed in his experimentation that the castle could catch on fire and burn around him and he'd barely notice.

She turned right at the top of the ramp and tiptoed to her old cell. Then she quietly lowered to her hands and knees and used an old spoon to pry up the loose floorboard beneath her cot, where she had hidden some of the more potent poisons she'd concocted from the herbs from her cemetery garden.

She lifted out a jug of fog juice and nodded to herself. "This'll stop Jack."

The saw whirred louder from the laboratory. Sally quickly replaced the floorboard. She knew it was safest to hurry down the ramp and get out of the castle, but her curiosity got the better of her. What experiment was the doctor working on now? She'd overheard the monsters in town whispering about Finkelstein's bold new project but had no idea what it was.

Hugging the jug of fog juice, she tiptoed to the open laboratory door and carefully peeked inside. Dr. Finkelstein was leaning over a new creation strapped down to the operating table. Sally could make out little more than a cadaver's bandaged skull.

"What a joy to think of all we'll have in common," the doctor purred to the bandaged cadaver. He lifted his skullcap, prodded around, and then teased out a good chunk of his brain matter and inserted it into the creation's empty skull. "We'll have conversations *worth* having."

Sally fought the urge to roll her eyes. That

silly old doctor. If conversation had been lacking in the past, it hadn't been Sally's fault. All Dr. Finkelstein ever wanted to talk about was electricity conduction.

He placed his hands on either side of the cadaver's skull and adjusted its head to fit just right on the neck joints. "Now then . . ."

Sally watched, partly in horror and partly in disgust, as the doctor leered toward his undead companion on the operating table, his lips pursed to press a cold kiss to her new brain. But as soon as he did, the cadaver's skullcap crashed down. The doctor's lips were smashed. He let out a wail.

Sally pressed a hand over her mouth, smothering her laugh. For both of their sakes, she hoped the doctor's new companion would be a better fit for him than she had ever been. She certainly had no intention of returning to servitude.

She tiptoed out of the castle, replaced the key beneath the gargoyle, and headed to the Town Square, determined to stop Jack.

CHAPTER SIXTEEN

CHRISTMAS EVE

BEYOND THE GATES of Halloween Town, the night grew cold and reeked of sulfur. As the bathtub marched through the gates and into the wilderness, Sandy Claws kicked at the bag, continuing to struggle. "Me, on vacation on Christmas Eve?"

The trick-or-treaters rolled their eyes. They were growing tired of his complaints.

"Where are we taking him?" Barrel asked Lock.

"Yeah, where?" Shock repeated.

Lock took off his mask and declared, "Why, to

Oogie Boogie, of course. There isn't anywhere in the world more comfortable than that." He gave a sly wink to Shock. "Jack said to make him comfortable, didn't he?"

"Yes, he did," Shock and Barrel agreed equally slyly.

From inside the sack, Sandy's muffled voice admonished them. "Haven't you heard of peace on Earth and goodwill toward men?"

"No!" The three trick-or-treaters erupted into cackles.

They led the walking bathtub up a rickety ramp into their tree house. Once they were in the main room, they let Sandy Claws out of the bag. He took a deep breath.

"Don't do this!" he protested. "Naughty children never get any presents."

That only made them laugh harder. What did they care about presents? It was the *act* of being naughty that was the true gift.

They stuffed him headfirst into the chute that led down to Oogie Boogie's lair. They cackled as they prodded his backside with a plunger, a broom, and a pitchfork. The big man kicked his little feet uselessly.

"I think he might be too big." Shock smacked his bottom with her broom.

"No, he's not," Lock disagreed. "If he can go down a chimney, he can fit . . . down . . . here!"

The three of them shoved their tools against his ample bottom, and with a cry, Santa Claus finally was squeezed into the chute. The metal pipes groaned as the large man tumbled down, popping nails and threatening to burst the pipes, until at last he spilled out into the dark abyss below.

He let out a hoarse yell as he landed with a thud on a circular table decorated with spikes. *Oh, those naughty children!* They had bound his hands with rope, and he felt like a Christmas roast ready for the fork.

Garish lights shone at one end of the dark cave. Santa squinted, trying to see his surroundings. The color of the room was a harsh neon blue, like nothing in his realm of white snow, green fir trees, and red candy canes. These phosphorescent lights reminded him of the plankton and blind fish that lived in the dark deep. Slimy, banished things. As the neon lights grew brighter, Santa blinked a few times. Shapes of skulls and flames began to take form in the darkness. They looked like parts of a game of cards or checkers, but nothing like the sweet versions his elves made. *These* games weren't made for children.

A burst of purple light shone on the cave floor.

Doors painted with glow-in-the-dark grinning skulls opened, and two dice clattered out. They skittered across the floor until they hit Santa's beard, then rolled to a stop on the ground next to him.

A sickly green light poured out of the chute overhead like a spotlight, illuminating a figure striding into the cave. Santa watched warily. Who was this fellow? He was as big as Santa himself but appeared to be nothing more than a burlap sack roughly stitched together into the shape of a person with only a vague suggestion of hands and feet. Uneven rips in the burlap sack served as eyes and a mouth.

"Well, well, well. What have we here?" Oogie Boogie asked.

His deep cackle echoed off the cave walls.

There was a reason Oogie Boogie stuck to his underground lair beyond the town gates. He was so vile that even the other monsters shuddered at his presence. There had been a time when he'd tried to take over Halloween Town and crown himself the Bug King, but his creepy-crawly henchmen had made a mess of everything, stealing everyone's candy corn and leaving the pumpkins to rot. Now he was king of nothing but a festering hole.

Oogie Boogie shimmied into the neon-green spotlight. "Sandy Claws? Oh, I'm scared!"

He pressed his cloth arms to his burlap cheeks as he opened his mouth in an exaggerated wail, showing off the worms that wriggled in his gums instead of teeth. Bugs tumbled out of his open mouth and landed on Santa's beard, burrowing their way into the thick white hair.

As the lights grew brighter, Santa saw that the tacky neon decorations in Oogie Boogie's lair weren't symbols from board games but rather games of chance. *Gambling! Oh, what a dirty vice!* Santa's elves would never make toys that encouraged gambling. He'd never dream of putting poker sets or toy slot machines under the tree.

But this living burlap sack clearly felt differently. In fact, Santa realized that the circular round table beneath him wasn't a table at all but part of a giant roulette wheel. Nearby, three slot machines lit up in bright colors and gave off clinking coin sounds.

What poor taste in decor! Santa thought. The whole place was a cross between a torture chamber and a casino, and all of it stank of mold.

Oogie Boogie, with his lumpy body, sashayed around the roulette wheel, laughing huskily. He set the round table spinning, and Santa moaned as the world spun in flashing bright blues and greens.

As soon as the table stopped, Oogie Boogie grabbed Santa by the tip of his beard and pulled him up until they were face to face. He leaned over him, letting a spider that was hanging off the tip of his head dangle an inch above the Christmas King's nose.

"I'm a gambling man, Mr. Claws. I live by the roll of the dice . . . and you will, too!"

Wrapping his baggy arms around Santa, he swung the large man in a series of dizzying spins as the lights flashed and seedy music played from the shadows. A yellow-and-black-striped snake slithered out of his mouth; it was all he had for a tongue.

Santa put on his sternest face. He wasn't much of a dancer, and he certainly didn't want this burlap figure as a partner. "Let me go at once. There will be a lot of disappointed children if I don't get free."

Oogie Boogie howled a laugh at the ceiling of his cave, and it set loose a flock of neon-winged bats.

"Oh, you are too much! I'm shaking!" He let go of Santa and pranced around his cavern, rattling chains and crunching bones in a torture press, and then grabbed a hook dangling from the ceiling. He was relishing having something to toy with besides grubs, and he fully intended to get all the merrymaking he could out of this plump visitor. "You aren't going anywhere, old man."

He strung the hook between Santa's bound hands and turned a crank that lifted the Christmas King into the air on a rope, swinging him around the multicolored spotlights dancing throughout the cave.

"I command you to release me!" Santa ordered.

Oogie Boogie knocked his baggy fist on the edge of the chute that led up to his minions' tree house. "Hear that, boys? He wants free."

The cackles of Lock, Shock, and Barrel carried down the chute, spilling into the cavern, where they echoed forbiddingly.

Oogie Boogie lowered the dangling Santa Claus until he could grab the man's white beard and pulled him right up to the hollow rips and tears he called a face. The monster reeked of bugs and rot.

"You ain't going nowhere," Oogie Boogie said with a throaty cackle. "You and me, we're going to play a game."

CHAPTER SEVENTEEN

CHRISTMAS EVE

CHRISTMAS EVE had arrived: the night every monster in Halloween Town had waited fourteen long months for.

In celebration, the Undead Ensemble played a rousing version of "Here Comes Sandy Claws" while the two-faced Mayor, wearing a poinsettia blossom pinned to his suit, conducted. For years he'd been reelected on the promise of delivering the greatest Halloween scares of all time, but this year—*ho!* This year had been a real challenge with Jack's whole Christmas thing. Still, he felt confident that night would be a legendary success, which he would be sure to remind his constituents of at election time.

The crowd's energy crackling in the air seemed different from the holiday eves of the past. This Christmas Eve there were no masks, no dripping blood, no severed heads—except the one the Undersea Gal had packaged up in a nice black bow for some little girl or boy to open under the tree.

While everyone was tapping their feet to the music and speculating about when Jack would make his grand appearance, Sally crept along the low stone wall surrounding the Town Square with the jug of fog juice clutched to her chest. Oh, how she hoped no one would see her. It would break her heart if Jack found out *she* was the reason his Christmas was about to become an utter failure. He wouldn't understand it now, but she was doing what was best for him.

She reached the fountain and uncorked the jug, then poured the contents into the bubbling green slime. Fortunately, the musical performance distracted everyone from the thick gray fog that oozed out and spilled down the sides of the fountain.

Back in the center of the square, the Mayor waved his hand toward the coffin sleigh, which was parked on the wooden ramp. At his signal, its door creaked open. Jack appeared from inside with his arms crossed grimly over his ribs as though he was rising from the dead. He wore the red suit Sally had made for him along with Sandy Claws' stocking cap.

The crowd cheered at their holiday king's clever entrance; he'd outdone himself again!

Even though she felt his plan was foolhardy, Sally couldn't help smiling. Jack loved to make a grand entrance even more than the Mayor did.

Sally slipped into the rear portion of the bystanders, nodding along as though she'd been there the entire time. Not far away, thick smoke from her fog juice potion spilled out of the fountain. The fountain was connected underground to the wishing well at the far end of the square, where even morc fog poured out.

The Mayor climbed onto the wooden ramp, which served as a makeshift stage. With his rosy face on proud display, he unfurled the speech he'd been working on for weeks and turned toward Jack. "Think of us as you soar triumphantly through the sky, outshining every star!"

Jack tipped up his chin, basking in the praise.

"Your silhouette a dark blot on the moon," the Mayor effused, dramatically throwing his hands in the air. "You who are our pride, you who are our glory, you who have frightened billions into an early grave!"

Jack's rib cage swelled with joy. None other than he, the Pumpkin King, could have achieved this: not only making Christmas his own, but improving it and even giving Sandy Claws a much-deserved rest as part of the bargain. He couldn't wait to hear the delighted laughter of children opening their presents on Christmas morning. Everyone would marvel over the extra-special changes he'd implemented that year.

A low but thick cloud of fog began to settle into the Town Square. Fog was nothing new in Halloween Town, so few residents paid it any bother, though it was rising unusually fast.

The members of the Undead Ensemble began to cough. A puff of fog even slipped out of the saxophone, and the sax player grumbled.

The Mayor held the scroll close and squinted at the writing to see. "You who have, eh, devastated the souls of the living . . ."

The crowd began to take more notice of the fog as it swallowed feet and legs. This was starting to seem unlike normal late-evening fog. The cobblestone streets had completely disappeared, and fog continued to pour out of the fountain and wishing well at an alarming rate.

"Oh, no!" Jack moaned as the fog rose to chin level. "We can't take off in this! The reindeer can't see an inch in front of their noses!"

The three skeletal reindeer hitched to his coffin sleigh weren't even visible through the thick cloud other than a faint gleam of their bones in the moonlight.

As the other monsters began to murmur worrisomely to themselves, Sally wiped the back of her hand over her forehead. "Whew!" Her plan had worked. Now her terrifying vision wouldn't come true, and Jack would be safe.

One of the vampires wailed, "This fog's as thick as . . . as . . ."

"Jellied brains!" the Cyclops interjected.

"Thicker!" cried another vampire. He should know. He'd had jellied brains for dinner just the night before.

Jack sank onto the driver's seat of his coffin sleigh and rested his weary chin on his hand in dejection. "There go all of my hopes, my precious plans, my glorious dreams."

Through the haze, he could barely make out the disappointed faces of the monsters gathered around the sleigh, though he heard the Corpse Kid say sullenly to his mother, "There goes Christmas!"

Desolate cries spread among the residents.

Somewhere in the haze, Zero barked. At first Jack couldn't see the ghost dog, who had the misfortune of being the same color as the fog itself.

Sadly, Jack shook his head. Wherever Zero was, it wasn't time for fetch. "No, Zero. Down, boy."

A strange warm orange glow was cast by an orb of light somewhere in the middle of the fog, capturing Jack's attention. He cocked his skull, curious. As the orb floated closer, he realized it was his ghost dog's pumpkin nose.

"My, what a brilliant nose you have," Jack observed, and then, seeing how the dog's glowing nose lit up the nearby faces of the crowd, which had previously been obscured, he grew more animated. "The better to light my way! To the head of the team, Zero!"

The dog's ghostly body fluttered with pride as he glided to the front of the harnessed reindeer.

As Zero's glowing nose grew bright enough to light up the entire crowd, they began to clap thunderously.

Christmas was saved! Tragedy averted!

Everyone was thrilled except for Sally, who pressed her palms against her face, shaking her head. *Oh, no!*

"We're off!" With a crack of his whip, Jack took his position at the head of the coffin sleigh and spurred on the cadaverous steeds. The reindeers' skulls broke into toothy smiles. Hooves dancing over the ramp, they followed Zero's nose like a beacon in the darkness. The sleigh lurched forward, and Jack, exhilarated, clutched the reins and gave the crowd a heartfelt wave.

The monsters shouted and cheered, urging him on. Every last ghost, zombie, and vampire wished they could be in that sleigh with the Pumpkin King. After all, in years past, the majority of them had been part of the scaring party that traipsed into the land of the living to bring about a frightful Halloween. But this year, Jack alone would represent the town for Christmas. Over a year of wrapping boxes and weaving garlands . . . and to think that at the last moment, it almost hadn't happened because of that unlucky fog. Thank goodness for Zero!

"Wait, Jack, no!" Sally yelled as the sleigh pulled forward on the ramp. The memory of her awful vision clung to her like rot. The orange glow of Zero's nose looked eerily similar to the flames that had engulfed the enchanted Christmas tree in her vision. But Jack couldn't hear her above the cheering crowd, no matter how loudly she yelled.

The monsters gasped as the sleigh rose into thin air. Dr. Finkelstein had done it! The reindeer flew! A large barrel in the rear of the coffin sleigh held all their handcrafted gifts for the children. They watched in delight as the sleigh soared higher and higher toward the yellow moon.

Jack's deep voice rang out clear as a bell. "Ho, ho, ho! Ha, ha, ha!"

Once the sleigh was out of sight, and with it the glowing light from Zero's nose, the town was plunged back into thick fog. Now that the initial excitement was over, the residents began to find their way through the fog to Town Hall, where the witch sisters had set up a scrying cauldron in which they could watch Jack's midnight run.

Sally remained alone in the Town Square, swallowed by her own fog, with her hands clutched to her chest and her chin tipped toward the sky.

"Goodbye, Jack. My dearest Jack." She'd done her best to prevent him from leaving, but the fog juice hadn't been enough. "Oh, how I hope my premonition was wrong."

She moved away from the thick fog but didn't go to Town Hall to celebrate with the others. The Undead Ensemble had taken up their usual place by the cemetery gates and were playing a lovely slow dirge. She ran her soft fingers along the cemetery wall as she listened to the melody.

"I sense there's something in the wind," she whispered.

A raspy meow stole her thoughts. A scruffy black cat slunk along the top of the wall and jumped down to wind between Sally's ankles.

She sighed as she spoke her fears aloud to the cat. "Jack didn't listen. Now he's out there, somewhere, and I'm afraid of what will happen."

Through the lingering fog, the cat trotted alongside the rag doll as she strolled toward the morose music playing in the distance. "I wish I could be celebrating with everyone, but I can't stop thinking about my vision. I think tonight is doomed."

She leaned against the cemetery's creaky gates and then let herself slide down to the scratchy grass. The cat nuzzled her, begging for attention.

She stroked it gently, thinking of Jack.

"Will we ever end up together?" she wondered aloud.

It seemed as though any romance between Jack and her was not meant to be. She'd done as much as she could for him, like that little fairy she'd once thought of herself as, but he hadn't taken notice of her feelings. Maybe his heart belonged to another, or maybe it was simply not meant to be for the Pumpkin King and the rag doll.

She nudged the cat into her lap, stroking it softly as she listened to the distant sounds of celebration. Her empty chest felt strangely heavy for one that didn't contain a heart.

Then the cat sprang out of her lap and ran away, leaving her alone once again.

She sighed heavily.

"No, I think not."

CHAPTER EIGHTEEN

CHRISTMAS EVE

JACK AND the skeletal reindeer soared above the clouds, following Zero's bright nose. The wind was fierce, but Jack cracked the whip, and the reindeer pushed on harder. He lifted a hand to his eyes to look for signs of life below. *Ah, yes!* A human town began to take shape beneath the clouds. He steered the reindeer lower until their hooves nearly brushed the rooftops as they glided along in the air. These were the same houses he had lovingly terrorized on Halloween year after year, but this time he had come to deliver joy.

"Ho-ho-ho! He-he-he!"

I'm really getting the hang of this Santa thing, he thought.

He skillfully guided the reindeer to land on a snow-covered rooftop, though their undead hooves slipped on the ice and they crashed into a collection of lit-up plastic angels, which fell off the roof with a clatter and dangled from a single nail.

Well, maybe a little *more practice.*

Jack dismounted with considerably more grace than the sleigh had landed with, and hefted the unwieldy bag of toys onto his shoulder. How did old Sandy Claws do it with his bad back? Jack felt that he was much better suited for the job. He slid down the chimney with ease and tugged the sack down after him.

Inside the house, a small child in an upstairs bedroom awoke at the clatter. The little boy blinked, rubbing his eyes before he remembered: it was Christmas! That clatter had to be Santa! The boy climbed out of bed and tiptoed down the stairs with Christmas spirit tingling throughout his body. He couldn't believe his eyes. A figure in a red suit leaned over the Christmas tree as he unpacked a sack of presents. The boy watched, mouth agape, as the figure filled his family's stockings hung over the fireplace.

"Santa?" the boy asked in wonder.

Jack whirled around.

A child! he thought. This was his chance. He reminded himself that this wasn't Halloween and he wasn't here to scare anyone. Instead, he gave his best toothy smile. "Merry Christmas! And what is your name?" He tapped the boy on the nose.

The boy couldn't take his eyes off the deathly pale shade of Santa's skin. In fact, it wasn't just pale. It was bone white. Or rather, it *was* bone . . .

"Uh . . . uh . . ." The boy was beginning to wonder if he was still asleep, because this Santa looked less like the jolly man from the North Pole and more like something out of his worst nightmares.

"That's all right!" Jack exclaimed in his jolliest voice. Clearly, the boy was so starstruck to see him that he'd lost his voice. "I have a special present for you anyway. There you go, sonny."

He reached into his sack and handed the boy a box wrapped neatly with a black satin bow, and with a wink of his eyeless socket, he launched himself backward up the chimney with a gleeful "Ho, ho, ho, he, he, he!"

Alone in his living room, the boy stared at the box. As alarming as his visit with Santa had been, a present was still a present. He unwrapped the package apprehensively as he heard the soft footsteps of his parents coming up behind him.

"And what did Santa bring you, honey?" asked his mother.

The boy peered into the box. He would have screamed if what he saw there hadn't been less frightening than the nightmarish *thing* dressed in a Santa suit that had delivered it.

He pulled out a shrunken head.

Across town, hundreds of children awoke to the sound of hooves on their roofs. Some noticed a strange *clackety-clack* sound of bones but decided to overlook that in their excitement. The children dashed to their Christmas trees and tore open the presents they had eagerly awaited all year.

Screams rang out from house to house.

Lights came on in each of the windows as parents woke in a cold sweat. Confused dogs barked at the spindly shadows flying high in the sky.

Far above town, Jack didn't hear the screams. All he heard were the cheers he imagined would be greeting him when he returned to Halloween Town in victory.

"Ho-ho-ho! Ha-ha-ha-ha!" he cried in joy, oblivious to the reign of terror he was spreading.

In one house, he left a man-eating holly wreath that came alive as soon as he left.

In another house, a twenty-foot snake slithered out of Jack's sack while his back was turned to fill the stockings.

Shortly after he departed the next house, a brother and sister awoke and eagerly scampered to the toy duck and teddy bear Jack had left them, throwing their arms around their gifts, only to flee in terror when the dolls bared sharp teeth and chased them around the house.

"Mom! Dad! Help!"

"Ahhhh!"

"Santa, why?"

In police stations across the globe, phones began to ring.

"Hello? Police," a receptionist said. "Attacked by Christmas toys? That's strange. That's the second toy complaint we've had."

Word soon spread of the nightmare terrorizing Christmas. A Santa imposter was delivering demonic toys! Parents began to shove sofas and buffet tables in front of their chimneys to block the

Santa imposter from entering. They bolted their fireplace guards with iron pokers. They turned up the gas so flames would destroy anything that tried to come down the chimney.

High up on the rooftops, Jack imagined the joyful scenes that must be taking place inside all the homes he had visited. Warmth spread through his cold, desiccated heart. This would be a Christmas no one would forget!

"You're welcome!" he called to the town far below. "One and all!"

Meanwhile, unbeknownst to Jack, phones continued to ring in police stations throughout the world faster than the receptionists could answer.

"Where'd you spot him? Fast as we can, ma'am."

"Police . . . I know, a skeleton. Keep calm. Turn off all the lights. Make sure the doors are locked."

"Hello? Police . . ."

Back in Halloween Town, the townsfolk watched one of the news programs as it was broadcast into the witches' scrying cauldron. The newscaster's face appeared thin and wan in the murky potion.

"Reports are pouring in from all over the globe that an imposter is shamelessly impersonating Santa Claus, mocking and mangling this joyous holiday."

The monsters burst into cheers. Good old Jack! He had spread nightmares throughout the land of the living once again! The little boys and girl must be thrilled!

While the witches and zombies congratulated themselves on another successful night, Sally leaned over the cauldron's edge to listen to the rest of the report.

The newscaster continued gravely, "Police assure us that at this moment, military units are mobilizing to stop the perpetrator of this heinous crime."

Sally pressed a hand to her cheek. "Jack! Someone has to help Jack."

The two-faced Mayor was standing at her side, but he hadn't heard the rest of the report. No one had. They were all overcome with excitement.

Sally gripped the edges of the cauldron. If none of the other townsfolk would help Jack, then it was up to her. She hadn't been able to detain Jack with her fog juice, and now her terrifying vision was coming true. If she didn't find a way to stop him before he delivered any more presents, then Christmas was going to end in flames, just like in her vision.

She didn't have much time.

Determinedly, she pushed through the celebrating crowd as she cried aloud, "Where'd they take that Sandy Claws?"

Back in the land of the living, Jack was making excellent time on his Christmas flight when, to his surprise, wide beams of light shone up at him. He peered down at the town far below, scratching his skull. The beams swept back and forth just like the Mayor's swinging spotlight in the Town Hall auditorium. That was it: spotlights! The people below were trying to catch glimpses of Christmas' latest celebrity.

"Look, Zero, searchlights!"

He grinned proudly. He was no stranger to the spotlight and knew how to play to his audience. He steered the sleigh in a little daredevil spin.

Fireworks exploded from below.

"They're celebrating!" Jack threw his arms in the air as more fireworks burst in the heavy clouds around them. "They're thanking us for doing such a good job."

He was feeling particularly pleased with himself when a firework exploded frighteningly close to the sleigh. Zero squealed in alarm and fluttered away just in time to avoid being toasted like a marshmallow.

"Whoa, careful down there! You almost hit us!" Jack called down. He shook his head. In their excitement, the people setting off the fireworks weren't paying attention to what they were doing. Without meaning to, they might accidentally harm the very person they were trying to celebrate!

Zero yipped a warning, looking pointedly at Jack.

"It's okay, Zero," Jack said reassuringly. "Head higher!"

He tugged on the reins, and the sleigh pulled upward, deeper into thick clouds, where they were hidden from the blasts.

Putting the fireworks out of his mind, Jack consulted the list of names on Sandy's scroll. "Who's next on my list? Ah, little Harry and Jordan. Won't they be surprised?"

As the wind shifted, the cloud cover broke apart, and Jack peered down at the snow-covered rooftops and twinkling decorations. A sudden spotlight blinded him. He recoiled, shading his face with his hand. Those silly people were *still* trying to catch a glimpse of their star!

Jack was starting to lose his patience with all the attention. If they kept up these spotlights and fireworks, he'd never finish his job by morning. As the clouds continued to thin, more spotlights zoned in on the sleigh.

The next firework soared up so fast that Jack couldn't steer away in time. The firework slammed into one of the reindeer. Its bones shattered apart and rained down.

Jack gasped and grabbed the reins to keep the other reindeer on track. But immediately, a second firework collided into the wooden barrel of toys. The barrel burst into flame. The sleigh tipped and rocked precariously, threatening to turn over. Jack struggled to grab as many flaming toys as he could salvage while trying to right the sleigh.

A flaming doll in his left hand singed his finger bones, and he gasped again as a terrible realization overcame him: they wanted Jack in flames, just like the doll!

"They're *trying* to hit us!"

Oh, what a mess of things! Didn't they understand? He was trying to spread cheer. To make the children laugh and smile!

"Zero!" he wailed.

Now he understood what his ghost dog had been trying to warn him of. If only he'd listened! Was this what Sally had been trying to warn him of, too?

Zero barked and whined as another firework zipped toward them.

They aren't fireworks, Jack thought. *They're missiles!*

The latest missile hurtling toward them collided with the bottom of the sleigh. The entire contraption shattered. The coffin the townspeople had worked so hard on splintered into pieces. Dr. Finkelstein's reindeer broke into bones. Toys were thrown into the air, and so was Jack.

As Jack fell through the clouds toward a ground that was rushing up to meet him, he cried out in a mournful wail, "Merry Christmas to all, and to all a good night!"

The sleigh and its passenger crashed to Earth like a falling star, leaving a smoking crater in its wake.

Back in Halloween Town, the townsfolk watched the events unfold in the witches' scrying cauldron. Their gasps were soon followed by tears. None of them could believe what they'd just witnessed with their own eyes, but it was undeniable. The impossible had happened. It wasn't one of Jack's clever tricks this time. Their Pumpkin King was gone.

The Wolfman howled his anguish up at the moon.

"I knew this Christmas thing was a bad idea," the Mayor lamented. "I felt it in my gut."

He climbed into his hearse and picked up his megaphone to break the tragic news to the rest of the town.

"Terrible news, folks. The worst tragedy of our times. Jack has been blown to smithereens. Terrible, terrible news!"

CHAPTER NINETEEN

CHRISTMAS EVE

"ARE YOU A gambling man, Sandy?" Deep in his lair, Oogie Boogie shook a pair of dice in the chubby Christmas King's face close enough to tickle his beard. "Let's play."

Garish neon lights shone on the walls of Oogie Boogie's underground hovel. The sounds of dinging slot machines and whirling roulette tables were deafening. Dangling from the end of a rope tied around his hands, Santa Claus wasn't sure how much more torture he could endure.

Right as Oogie Boogie prepared to throw the dice, a knock at his door made him pause. Who could it be? Visitors were unheard of in his lair. Even Lock, Shock, and Barrel refused to come down from their tree house into the pit. Oogie Boogie was usually alone with his bugs and the occasional snake.

A shapely female leg slipped between the jagged gaps in his lair's door. The owner of the leg remained coyly hidden as though too shy to reveal herself. A dainty black boot lifted into the air tantalizingly.

The cloth that formed Oogie Boogie's lips fell open in shock.

His first visitor . . . and *what* a visitor!

"Mmm! My, my, what have we here?" With a wiggle of his burlap eyebrows, he spit into his hand and swiped back the unruly top of his sack head before sauntering toward the door.

The leg gave an extra-alluring shimmy.

As Oogie Boogie traipsed toward the leg, two disembodied cloth hands crawled through the barred window high up on the opposite side of the cave. Sally had never been so thankful for a body that could come apart with a simple tug of thread. Her hands had a mind of their own, but luckily, all her various parts agreed on the same thing: only Sandy Claws could save Jack now.

While Sally's leg distracted Oogie Boogie, her hands pushed themselves off the wall and grabbed on to the rope holding up Sandy Claws. They used their fingers to climb down the rope silently. One of her hands clamped itself over Sandy's mouth before he could scream. The other pointed upward urgently.

Santa Claus followed the hand's indicated direction to see Sally outside the barred window. Her arms, which ended in stumps packed with dry leaves, clung to the bars.

"I'll get you out of here," she whispered as loudly as she dared.

Her disembodied hands made quick work of untying the knot that bound Santa's hands.

Meanwhile, Sally unrolled a rope ladder she had attached to the window.

As quietly as he could, Santa tiptoed to the ladder and began to climb.

Back at the lair's jagged door, Sally's leg was still teasing Oogie Boogie with its coy dance.

"Ah, lovely," Oogie Boogie's deep voice rumbled. He ran his sack hand down the curve of the leg and tossed off its black boot with a flourish.

"Tickle, tickle, tickle," he teased as he toyed with the bottom of the foot. What a delightful visitor this was! He'd booby-trapped his lair with all sorts of mechanical devices to keep unwanted guests out, but for this lovely lady, he'd gladly make an exception . . .

Oogie Boogie pulled a little too hard, and to his confusion, the leg came away in his hands. He stumbled back in outrage as he looked at the detached rag doll leg spilling dried leaves.

"What?" he roared. He whirled around to find Sandy Claws and Sally making their escape out

the window. Now he understood the trick that rag doll had played on him with her detached leg. "You trying to make a dupe out of me?"

He drew in a deep breath powerful enough to suck up dozens of wriggling and crawly bugs around the lair. The force of his inhale even threatened to pull Sandy off the ladder. The old man clutched the rung with all his strength, but Oogie Boogie's lungs were too strong. The rope ladder tore clear off the window, dragging Sandy Claws as well as Sally back into the lair.

Sally and Santa Claus were so dazed by their fall that it didn't take Oogie Boogie long to capture the two of them. He threw Sally into his iron maiden torture chamber, while he tied down Santa to a portion of the roulette wheel that was angled up like a plank. Sally took her needle from her hair, where she had hidden it, and quickly sewed on her disembodied hands and leg before Oogie Boogie dragged her out and tied her down on the plank next to Sandy.

Oogie Boogie stood over them and cackled huskily. Try to get one over on him? Not today! Now he was especially glad he'd booby-trapped his lair, because these two visitors were *definitely* unwelcome.

"You wait till Jack hears about this!" Sally cried. "By the time he's through with you, you'll be lucky if you—"

Her threat was interrupted by the sound of the Mayor's megaphone coming from somewhere outside. The Mayor's voice filtered through the window. "The king of Halloween has been blown to smithereens! Skeleton Jack is now a pile of dust!"

Oogie Boogie's cloth mouth pulled back into a devilish grin. This was the best news he'd heard in months! He rattled a pair of dice in his hand. "What's that you were saying about luck, rag doll?"

Santa Claus shook his head in sorrow.

Sally gasped. *Not Jack!*

In the land of the living, Jack Skellington lay broken and battered on a cold gray statue, surrounded by snow and fire.

A policeman's voice cut through the night on a nearby patrol car's speaker. "Attention, citizens. Terrible news. There's still no sign of Santa Claus. Although the imposter has been shot down, it looks like Christmas will have to be canceled this year. I repeat, the imposter has been shot down, but there's still no sign . . ."

The voice faded as the police car turned down a road that took it in the other direction. To Jack, the words came as though in a half-forgotten dream.

Imposter . . . Canceled . . . Shot down . . .

Was he dead—again? The first time he'd died had been so long ago that he couldn't even recall what had killed him. Ah, well, whatever it had been, it couldn't possibly have been worse than this.

This death was icy cold.

It was darkly bleak.

It was . . .

A faint bark made him blink his eye sockets open.

Maybe I'm not dead after all, he thought, *though I might as well be.*

He looked around to discover that he was sprawled in the middle of a snow-covered cemetery. Gravestones rose like petrified dragon scales out of the shadows. Pieces of the broken sleigh were scattered everywhere.

Zero floated over with Jack's jawbone clutched in his mouth, and affixed it back onto Jack's skull. Even though Zero and Jack had survived the crash, Zero's nose had lost its glow, as the dog felt the depths of his friend's sorrow.

Jack tested out his jawbone to make sure it worked. He sat up slowly on the large tablet-like open book held out by a stone angel who had broken his fall. His Sandy Claws suit was in tatters. Soot streaked his face. Broken bones would heal, but how would he ever repair the damage he'd done to the world?

All around the cemetery, the ruins of the sleigh smoldered in the snow. The toys his town's residents had spent months crafting were quickly becoming nothing but ash. How fitting that his flight should end in a cemetery, where his greatest hopes would be buried forever.

"What have I done?" he moaned.

He rested his skull in his hands, feeling the weight of the world on his shoulders. How could he have been so wrong? How had everything ended up such a mess? All he'd wanted was to show them something they'd never seen before—to dazzle them.

He flopped back onto the angel statue's open book with a hand pressed against his forehead.

Poor Jack, he thought, pitying himself.

"Bury me, Zero," he moaned. "I want to be dead and gone."

He could picture his headstone now:

HERE LIES

POOR OLD JACK

Zero floated aimlessly around his companion as the wrecked toys continued to smolder. He didn't even pick up a piece of a broken tricycle for fetch.

Jack sighed deeply. "Oh, well. I tried, didn't I?"

Then he suddenly sat up again. The rising flames and the cool night air were stirring his bones back to life.

Yes. He *had* tried—and he'd come so close! Who else could boast such a feat?

Zero's nose began to glow again, faintly.

As the spotlights continued to sweep overhead, Jack's spine straightened. "Yes, I tried. And you know what? For a while there, I *did* dazzle. I flew among the stars! And oh, the stories they'll have to tell their children. Tales of the most memorable Christmas ever!"

He curled his hand into a triumphant bony fist.

He jumped down from the statue, testing out his bruised bones as he strode among the flaming wreckage. "I'm starting to feel like myself again!"

He leapt onto a tombstone. His bones were starting to remember what it felt like to leap. To dance! He jumped from one gravestone to another, growing more excited. He had never been meant to spread *cheer*. He was meant to sow *terror*! To haunt children's dreams! To rouse goose bumps! He jumped on the back of a bench and let it fall backward as he gracefully sprang onto another statue. Then he ripped off the red suit to reveal his black-and-white-striped Halloween suit beneath.

He howled up at the night, "I'm Jack. The Pumpkin King!"

He cackled as he cavorted beneath the spotlights sweeping overhead. His bones had forgotten what they were for a short time, but now they remembered. He tested out a few of his old prizewinning scare faces.

I have the best ideas for all-new scares . . .

His arms stretched toward the moon as Zero floated over, holding the Santa hat in his jaw.

Jack's arms suddenly fell. All his renewed confidence moved aside in one fell swoop as he remembered everyone waiting for him back in Halloween Town. And there was no telling what those rascals Lock, Shock, and Barrel had done to poor old Sandy Claws. Jack needed to get to Oogie Boogie's lair before it was too late.

"Oh, no. I hope there's time to set things right!"

Tucking the Sandy Claws hat into his suit's inner pocket, he threw open a trapdoor at the feet of the angel statue and dove into a dark tunnel within.

"Come on, Zero," Jack called back to his dog. "Christmas isn't over yet!"

CHAPTER TWENTY

CHRISTMAS EVE

JACK AND ZERO rushed out of the tunnel to find themselves back in Halloween Town's cemetery. They charged through the gates, over hills, and around trees at the edge of the Hinterlands forest. In the distance, lights blazed in Oogie Boogie's lair. Jack felt an awful premonition in his bones.

"Help! Help!"

That was Sally's voice! Those little trouble-makers Lock, Shock, and Barrel hadn't taken good care of Sandy Claws at all. As Jack had feared, they'd taken him—and Sally, too!—straight to Oogie Boogie.

Jack raced across the unsteady bridge that led to the trick-or-treaters' tree house but stopped short when he heard Oogie Boogie's deep voice rumbling below.

He placed a finger to his mouth, hushing Zero.

"Looks like it's Oogie's turn to boogie now," Oogie Boogie said, cackling, within his lair.

Sally screamed.

Jack took hold of the rope that held up the elevator cage, and lowered himself until he could see into the pit. Oogie Boogie had constructed a makeshift roof out of tin paneling, with a few barred windows. Inside the lair, Sally and Sandy Claws were tied down to an angled plank. The center of the roulette wheel was open and revealed a fiery vat of magma. An enormous eight ball attached to clawlike rotating blades was poised over the lava, stirring it to keep it from hardening.

Jack continued to descend until he reached one of the lair's windows and squeezed his narrow frame through its iron bars.

Oogie Boogie rolled a pair of dice and clapped in ecstasy as they showed the numbers three and four. With both hands he grabbed a crank attached to the plank and began to pull it back.

"One, two, three," he said, cackling, as he cranked three times. The plank began to tilt. Sally and Sandy started sliding toward the vat of boiling lava, and Sally let out another wail.

Oogie Boogie sniggered as he cranked faster. "Four, five, six, seven!" The plank angled even more.

"This can't be happening!" Sandy Claws moaned.

Oogie Boogie let go of the crank and frolicked around the oversized roulette wheel like a schoolchild singing nursery rhymes. "Ashes to ashes and dust to dust. Oh, I'm feeling weak . . . with *hunger*! One more roll of the dice oughta do it."

As Oogie Boogie picked up his dice to throw again, Jack crept into the lair like a spider, silent and deadly, keeping to the shadows.

Oogie Boogie threw the dice. This time they landed in a skeleton's hollow skull, rolled down its throat, and tumbled out of its rib cage.

Oogie Boogie checked the numbers on the dice.

One.

One.

"*What?*" Oogie Boogie thundered in fury. "Snake eyes?"

There was no way two measly cranks was going to do the job. At that rate, his prisoners would die of old age before falling into the lava. Angry, he thumped his fist on the table hard enough to send the dice flying. When they settled again, new numbers showed.

"Eleven!" Oogie Boogie declared with a chortle. Now that was more like it. "Looks like I won the jackpot. Bye-bye, Dollface and Sandman."

He threw his weight against the lever, and the plank tipped dangerously. Sally screamed as she and Sandy lost their balance. They tried to hold on to the plank, but it was useless with their hands bound. They both slid toward the vat of lava and . . . disappeared.

Oogie Boogie guffawed as he prepared to revel in their screams. Jack wasn't the only one who could inspire a good shriek. The sound of screams was music to his ears . . .

He frowned.

For some reason, his victims' screams had stopped as soon as they had begun. His prisoners couldn't have died *that* fast. He'd thrown enough beetles into the vat to know that lava took a while to burn through a creature.

"What the—"

He peered into the vat but didn't see any sign of the rag doll or the bearded man. No bones. No red hair. Confused, he tilted the plank back up to see if something had gone wrong with the machinery underneath, and was flabbergasted to find a snappily dressed skeleton reclined on the other side.

Oogie Boogie recoiled in horror.

Jack Skellington! *That ghoul!* He must have somehow helped Sally and Sandy Claws escape before they fell into the vat and burned to death.

"Hello, Oogie," Jack said coolly.

"J-J-Jack!" Oogie Boogie clutched his baggy hands together as he backed away. "But they said you were dead. You must be . . ." He pretended to shiver in fright as he moved away from the skeleton. Then he slyly mashed his foot against a spider-shaped button that was hidden on the floor—another one of his tricks. *"Double dead!"*

"Oh!" Jack cried out as the roulette wheel began to rotate. Heat and flames flared up from the pit where Sally and Sandy had almost met their ends. Life-sized playing cards on mechanical springs popped up around the perimeter of the wheel, wielding sharp iron knives, trapping Jack. In the center, the eight ball's clawlike blades extended and spun like the churning mixer of a blender.

With spiderlike reflexes, Jack dropped to all fours, contorting to stay beneath the blades' reach.

Oogie Boogie pranced to the far side of the roulette wheel, laughing huskily as he taunted Jack. "Well, come on, Bone Man."

Oogie Boogie hadn't planned on having so many visitors that night—it was practically a soiree!—but he was game for a surprise. Especially if it meant he could slash and mash the Pumpkin King into pumpkin pie.

Zero barked ferociously outside the window to Oogie Boogie's lair.

At the sound of Zero's barking, Sally and Sandy Claws peeked out from behind the iron maiden torture device, where they had taken shelter.

Jack knew all about Oogie Boogie's love for games of chance, but he'd had no idea what exactly Oogie Boogie had spent years constructing down there in his underground lair. Oogie Boogie's roulette wheel was a cruel gauntlet designed by a rotten mind. The spinning wheel was rimmed with macabre symbols on the ball pockets: skulls mixed in with hearts, spades, and diamonds. Pumpkin-colored light emanated from the vat at the base of the wheel, and Jack kept slipping on the wheel's slope, sliding closer and closer to the lava.

The life-sized playing cards whirled their mechanical knives in a deadly onslaught. But Jack expertly judged the distance and leapt over each one with grace and cunning.

"Eh!" Oogie Boogie grunted, dismissing Jack's feats with a wave of his hand. Bored by Jack's ability to dodge his obstacles, he pulled a cord to transform the roulette wheel into an even deadlier game.

The playing cards lowered back into the rotating roulette base. Jack had to march fast to keep up with the wheel's speed so as not to be sucked into the lava.

In the dark recess of the cavern, three sets of red eyes glowed to life. Whoever they belonged to seemed even taller than Jack. The clanking and churning sounds of machinery grew louder as an installation of three slot machines, gliding forward on metal tracks, appeared out of the smoke. Each machine was topped with a skull with glowing eyes and had, instead of a lever to pull for a prize, a mechanical arm topped with a pistol.

"Fire!" Oogie Boogie ordered his machines.

The lair filled with the deafening sounds of clanking coins and bells. The robotic slot machines lowered their levers toward Jack. They fired. *Bam! Bam! Bam!* Jack sprang up from the spinning floor, his long legs arching over the gunshots.

Instead of running away from the armed slot machines, he charged them with a snarl, jumping right on top of their mechanical arms and dancing on them in a taunting jitterbug. They'd never shoot him now!

Oogie Boogie glowered in frustration; that skinless collection of bones was outsmarting his games of chance. Well, good thing he'd rigged all the games. The house always won, and this was *his* house.

Time to up the ante.

Oogie Boogie used the wheel's momentum to launch himself off the roulette floor with a gleeful "Whee!" As he flew off the wheel, he smacked his hand on a skull-shaped button. It was the trigger to launch a rotating saw from the ceiling. The saw's previous victim, nothing but bones now, was wired on to the saw like a stuntman on a carnival wheel.

The rotating saw arched down from the ceiling on a giant retractable arm, heading straight for Jack. Jack was so close to the loud gunshots of the slot machine that he didn't hear the saw bearing down on him.

Oogie Boogie danced from foot to foot in excitement as he watched the blade lower toward Jack. The pot was about to get a lot sweeter!

"Jack, look out!" Sally shouted.

At her cry, Jack turned and caught sight of the spinning blades closing in. He threw himself off the slot machines a second before the saw cut into them. Sparks flew everywhere. The pistols were sawn clean off, and clattered to the floor.

Jack landed on the spinning roulette wheel across from Oogie Boogie. He gave the Bug King his best Halloween scare face, and the festering sack flailed his arms in the air. But as soon as the shock wore off, Oogie Boogie slammed his hand down on one of the rigged roulette panels, which hid a secret springboard. It shot him upward, where he grabbed on to the pole holding the rotating clawlike blades, though in the commotion, a small string had caught from his burlap-sack body on a screw and now began to unravel.

"So long, Jack! Ha, ha, ha!" He waved his arms tauntingly as he laughed. The loose string dangled toward the games of chance.

"How dare you treat my friends so shamefully," Jack admonished him. He grabbed Oogie Boogie's fluttering string and gave it a taut tug.

To Oogie Boogie's horror, the string pulled loose from his burlap skin. His lumpy sack body had served him perfectly well, but now he was realizing that his stitches were much too loose and mostly composed of knots that easily unraveled with a simple tug.

The seam split open from the tip of his hand to his flappy underarm. Inside, hundreds of squiggly bugs wriggled in the sudden freedom.

Worms.

Beetles.

Spiders.

Grubs.

Moths.

Centipedes.

Every type of creepy-crawly beast in Halloween Town had been stuffed into that sack, and they clung together to make the creature called Oogie Boogie.

Oogie Boogie gave a few desperate cries as he tried to hold together the open seam. But bugs continued to spill out, tumbling down into the lava with tiny shrieks. The dangling string caught on the rotating blades beneath the eight ball and, before Oogie Boogie could free it, became a giant tangle. With a rip the entire burlap sack was sucked into the rotating blades.

Completely exposed, Oogie Boogie was nothing but a mass of writhing bugs. Thousands of them pulsated in the form of the Bug King, scrambling to maintain their shape but slipping and falling regardless.

Oogie Boogie dramatically raised a hand to his brow and clung to a rope with the other. "Now look what you've done!" Without his burlap skin, his face was nothing but gaping holes for his mouth and eyes and a striped purple beetle for a nose.

As the bugs lost their hold and fell, Oogie Boogie's shape began to diminish.

"My bugs!" he wailed. "My bugs . . ."

His throaty voice transformed into the high-pitched lament of hundreds of tiny cries as the creature that had been Oogie Boogie broke apart.

"My buuuugs . . . my buuuuuugs . . ."

Sally and Santa Claus came out from their hiding spot with mouths agape to behold the end of Oogie Boogie. Overhead, Zero found a gap in the windowsill and floated in, his nose shining brightly.

"Mmmyyy buuuugsssss . . ." A slimy green caterpillar wriggled across the floor only to end its miserable life smashed beneath Santa's heavy boot. Santa ground his boot into the cave floor with a grimace.

That's what you get, Santa thought, *for being naughty.*

After dusting himself off, Jack sheepishly handed the Christmas King his red cap. "Forgive me, Mr. Claws. I'm afraid I made a terrible mess of your holiday."

Santa gave Jack a look of paternal disapproval.

"Bumpy sleigh ride, Jack?" Santa snapped as he snatched his cap. "The next time you get the urge to take over someone else's holiday, I'd listen to her." He jabbed a finger toward Sally, who was lingering shyly behind the iron maiden. "She's the only one who makes any sense around this insane asylum!"

Sally smiled softly.

Grumbling to himself, Santa placed his red cap firmly over his scalp. His poor head had been chilled for hours. And Mrs. Claus would have baked him into a pie if he'd lost the cap she had knit for him!

Balling his fists and thinking of the long night's work ahead of him, he stomped toward the exit while grumbling, "Skeletons."

"I hope there's still time," Jack called after him.

Santa stopped abruptly and spun around. "To fix Christmas? Of course there is. I'm Santa Claus!"

He pressed his index finger to the side of his nose, gave Jack one more disapproving glare, and then, with a twinkle of magic, flew straight up into the air through Lock, Shock, and Barrel's chute. It was still snug, but with a little extra magic, he squeezed through.

Watching Sandy Claws disappear through the chute, Jack felt remorse and relief mingle together inside his rib cage. Everything would soon be back to how it should be, so why did he still get the sense that something was left unfinished?

Sally moved out of the shadows. "He'll fix things, Jack. He knows what to do." She touched his wrist gently.

Jack looked at her hand touching him and asked incredulously, "How did you get down here, Sally?"

A wave of shyness overcame her. She looked at her hands, toying with her soft fingers. "Oh, I was just trying to . . . well, I wanted to . . . to . . ."

"To help me?" Jack prompted.

She looked away as her phantom heart pattered faster in her chest. "I couldn't let you just . . ."

"Sally." Jack rested a bony hand on her shoulder and turned her gently toward him. He pressed his other hand against his chest. At last he was starting to form an inkling of what had been missing in his life. All this time he'd thought he'd simply grown bored with Halloween, but that hadn't been it at all.

He said, "I can't believe I never realized that you . . ."

They moved imperceptibly closer to each other as though drawn together by a string connecting them. Jack hadn't noticed that the thread on her face was a different color from the string that held together the rest of her body. Or that beneath her autumn-leaf scent, she also smelled of oleander. There was so much he didn't know about Sally, but he wanted to . . .

"Jack! Jack!"

Someone called from the barred window as a bright spotlight flooded down on them. Peering up into the light, Jack shaded his eyes. It was the Mayor of Halloween Town, along with Lock, Shock, and Barrel!

"Here he is!" Barrel cried.

"Alive!" Lock added.

"Just like we said," Shock insisted.

Holding the searchlight, the Mayor wore the smiling side of his face, but not even that maniacal grin could convey the depths of his excitement. Jack was back! He wasn't a broken pile of bones! The Mayor quickly lowered a rope. "Grab ahold, my boy!"

The knotted rope unrolled to the bottom of the cave. Jack clutched the rope with one hand and took Sally's hand with his other. She felt light in his grasp, like a dream.

The trio of troublemakers and the Mayor tugged on the rope with all their strength.

"Whoa!" Jack and Sally cried in unison as they were hoisted up to safety.

CHAPTER TWENTY-ONE

CHRISTMAS EVE

IN THE WORLD of the living, bulletins spread reports of the imposter's arrest and Santa Claus' return.

Broadcasters were anxious to put their listeners' fears to rest. "Good news, folks," reporters said. "Santa Claus, the one and only, has finally been spotted. Old Saint Nick appears to be traveling at supersonic speed. He's setting things right, bringing joy and cheer wherever he goes."

Santa Claus drove his team of reindeer swiftly from house to house, squeezing down chimneys to capture the demonic toys Jack had delivered and replace them with the sweet presents boys and girls had put on their lists.

He snatched up the evil jack-o'-lantern-in-the-box the witches had cursed to attack a husky boy in glasses and gave the child a candy cane instead.

He caught the possessed gunshot-ridden duck and flying vampire teddy, which had cornered the brother and sister in their bedroom, and left a toy sailboat and a stuffed pink bear in their place.

He took the shrunken head from the wide-eyed boy in plaid pajamas, whose parents had passed out from shock, and gave the child a waggly-tailed puppy wrapped up in a bow.

A newscaster continued, "Yes, folks, Kriss Kringle has pulled it out of the bag and delivered Christmas to excited children all over the world!"

The good news reflected in the witch sisters' scrying cauldron, but none of the Halloween Town residents heard it. The witches slumbered on the floor of their cottage. When they'd heard the tragic news of Jack's crash, they had burst into tears and prodded everyone out with their broomsticks. The monsters had shambled through town, wailing like banshees as they listened to the Mayor lament over his megaphone while he drove up and down the streets. Almost all the residents of Halloween Town cried themselves to sleep, from the Undersea Gal, asleep in the murky fountain water, to the vampires, hanging upside down in their attic. Only the Undead Ensemble still haunted the streets, with a dirge for the fallen Pumpkin King.

Now the witches twitched awake at the sound of a car horn honking emphatically.

They sat up, removing their eye masks to reveal eyes puffy and red from mourning. They exchanged looks. That horn sounded like it belonged to the Mayor's hearse. But instead of sobbing into his megaphone, now the Mayor was honking in excited bursts.

Could it be?

Could the Mayor have good news?

The witches tossed off their blankets and freshened up by rubbing extra dirt in their fingernail beds. They wanted to look their best in case Jack was back from the dead.

In town, the gatekeeper yawned awake and lit his lantern. When he saw the dark hearse bumping through the Hinterlands, he hurried to raise the gate. The sounds of honking and the excited speculation of townspeople carried through the streets, waking every resident of Halloween Town.

The Cyclops threw open his shutters on the top story of an angular stone cottage. From his vantage point, he could see the Mayor's car approaching the gate with several figures inside. "Jack!" he cried. "Jack's back!"

The Undersea Gal popped up from her slime bath in the fountain. She blew slime out of her gills. "Jack?"

The Winged Demon, who had just woken and was hanging upside down on the fountain's spout, threw open his wings. "Jack's okay!"

The Mayor's hearse joyfully chugged into the Town Square as sleepy residents woke, rubbed their eyes, hurried to pull on their clothes, and rushed out to meet the Mayor's hearse.

"He's all right!" cried the Creature Under the Stairs.

With Sally seated next to him, the Mayor parked in front of Town Hall and shut off the jack-o'-lantern-shaped headlights. Lock, Shock, and Barrel tumbled down from the top of the hearse, talking excitedly about their brave battle with Oogie Boogie to anyone who would listen. The Mayor immediately began shaking hands.

Sally remained in the front seat of the hearse, enjoying the excitement of the crowd.

Everyone only had eyes for Jack.

In his black pinstripe suit, Jack Skellington had never looked more dashing. He descended from the top of the hearse, bowed deeply to the crowd, and started up the steps to Town Hall. Laughter and joyous cries rang out around him.

The Corpse Kid clung to his leg, beaming up at him with his rotting smile. He'd told Jack on more than one occasion that he wanted to be just like him when he grew up, and Jack had assured the boy that his flesh would fall off his bones soon enough and he'd grow up to be a fine skeleton, too.

Jack reached the top of the stairs, where the Mayor was already waiting for him. Jack tossed the Corpse Kid into the air for good luck before placing him atop the Mayor's oversized hat, then gave the Mayor a solid handshake. The Mayor was always talking about them being a team; Jack had never felt prouder to call either one of his two faces a friend.

"It's great to be home!" Jack announced.

Everyone broke into applause. Jack beamed as he looked over his friends and neighbors. Yes, this was indeed where he belonged: among the dark, dismal, wonderfully terrifying creatures of the night. He would never again question his place in this eerie world.

Far in the distance, a deep "ho-ho-ho" carried on the wind.

The Halloween Town folk tipped their chins up toward the velvet black. The moon was fat and full. The silhouette of a sleigh and eight reindeer crossed its face.

"Happy Halloween!" Santa Claus called down to them.

Jack lifted a hand to wave and answered, "Merry Christmas!"

Jack was pleased to know there were no hard feelings. Holiday kings had to stick together, after all. He would never take over another holiday again, but there could come a time when he needed Sandy's help. One day he might be too sick to lead the scare team into the land of the living on October 31. Sandy Claws or that giant pink bunny might have to don a ghost costume and lead the haunting for him.

The night slowly filled with tiny white speckles. The townspeople gazed up in wonder. What were these bright spots? Were they stars? There had never been stars above Halloween Town before. Their nights were a thick, unbroken smear of black except for the light of the moon. But these stars were . . . *falling*. They fluttered down in icy waltzes.

"What's this?" the Corpse Kid asked, catching a flake in the rotting palm of his hand.

"What's this?" Dr. Hyde echoed, equally befuddled.

The Mayor stuck out his tongue to catch a flake. At the icy zap, his head immediately rotated to the happy side.

Despite none of the Halloween Town residents' ever having experienced snow, the magic in the air drew smiles on their faces. The townspeople began to frolic and play. The lake at the edge of town froze over into smooth ice, and the vampires pasted knife blades onto the bottoms of their shoes and wobbled onto the ice, skating around like happy, clumsy children. They used their umbrella handles like hockey sticks to pass a pumpkin back and forth.

At the edge of the lake, Behemoth and the Undersea Gal flopped onto their backs in a deep snowdrift and waved their arms and legs to make funny shapes; Behemoth thought they looked like angels in the snow, but the Undersea Gal scoffed and insisted the wide wings clearly made them snow bats.

A snowball flew through the air and smacked Jack right in his eye cavity. He sputtered in surprise and wiped away the snow. When he saw Lock, Shock, and Barrel giggling as they hid behind the frozen fountain, he tipped back his skull and laughed heartily. He couldn't stay mad at those scamps for long, even if they had caused trouble for him. Oogie Boogie was only a memory now, and as far as Jack was concerned, so was his ire. The simple truth was that Jack was exactly where he belonged. He was a creature of the night. A fearsome ghoul.

He, Jack Skellington, was the Pumpkin King.

Moving away from the crowd, Sally wandered to the gates outside Jack's house and plucked a thistle from the same clump she had admired before. She twirled it between her fingers, studying it closely in the snowfall, as she strolled through town. Oh, how she hoped there would be no more visions. No more fire—unless it was on a candle in a jack-o'-lantern.

The familiar whine of Dr. Finkelstein's wheelchair made her look up in surprise. The evil scientist, accompanied by the female creation he had been working on so diligently in his laboratory, wheeled into the Town Square.

"Careful, my precious Jewel," he purred to his companion.

Sally spied on them from a distance. She didn't run away this time. She was done fleeing. She had her sewing and had made good friends with the Hanging Tree. Besides, Dr. Finkelstein had a new companion now. The latest animated corpse was Sally's opposite in every way: the new assistant, dressed in an expensive fur stole and a pearl necklace, was all hard bone and freakish angles.

A female version of the doctor himself! Sally thought with a laugh.

From the opposite side of the Town Square, Jack also gaped at the appearance of Dr. Finkelstein and his uncanny female double.

Well, he's finally made his match, Jack thought. *Sally was never right for him. She is far too curious, too clever, too kind . . .*

Speaking of Sally, where was she?

Jack's chest swelled as he thought of the rag doll who had come to his rescue. When he'd seen her in danger in Oogie Boogie's lair, he had felt a slice of fear that cut far deeper than his concern for his other fellow citizens.

Sally had been there in the shadows so often, just behind the scenes, sprinkling magic dust to help him on whatever quest beckoned him. He recalled her delivering the basket of absinthe and provisions. Making his Sandy Claws costume. Sneaking into Oogie Boogie's lair to save Sandy Claws. She'd even tried to warn him, but he hadn't listened. What a fool he'd been. Would she ever forgive him?

He finally caught sight of her slipping through the town gates. Where was she going? Why wasn't she celebrating with everyone else? He'd made such a mess of things, but now all he desired was to tie up the final loose threads.

And there was one thing he still had to put right.

Sally climbed to the top of Spiral Hill, searching for a moment of respite away from the unruly partiers. She clutched the thistle in one hand. Fortunately, it hadn't burst into flame as part of another vision. It was simply a flower. She sighed to herself as she plucked off the petals in the moonlight.

He loathes me.

He loathes me not.

He loathes me.

He loathes me not . . .

She heard soft footsteps behind her and turned with a gasp.

It was Jack!

Jack Skellington had entered the cemetery and now stood at the bottom of Spiral Hill with a hand pressed to his chest.

"My dearest friend," he called up to her, "may I join you?"

Her stitched mouth tugged into a smile.

Jack climbed the snow-covered hill slowly, taking his time on this most important step of setting things right. At the top, he extended a bony hand to her.

She took his hand in her own cloth one.

For so long, she'd been shy around the Pumpkin King, but something seemed different now. Maybe it was that Christmas magic Jack was always talking about, or maybe it was a different kind of magic the two of them had summoned on their own.

She felt the tingle of another premonition—a lovely one this time.

"Come be with me, my dearest Jack," she whispered.

They clasped hands beneath the moon while Zero floated happily amid the icicles clinging to the underside of Spiral Hill.

"Sally, it's clear now that . . ." Jack started.

"We're simply meant to be," she finished.

They found each other in an embrace beneath the moon. Sally's cloth lips brushed a tender kiss against Jack's mouth. Her soft arms surrounded his angular shoulders. The snow had stopped falling, but Jack felt that the world now held more magic than ever before. He thought back to the previous Halloween, when all the cheers and merriment from another successful holiday hadn't bolstered his spirits as it reliably had in the past. He'd felt something was missing in his life, like a hole in his undead heart. But all that time, it wasn't change he'd been searching for. It wasn't a different holiday or a town with holly wreaths decorating front porches instead of jack-o'-lanterns. What he'd been desperately scouring the world for had been right in front of him the whole time. Sally had filled the hole in his heart with well wishes and delicious treats, and then she had mended that hole with her gentle courage.

Sally, unlike Jack, didn't spare a thought for the past as they held each other. She leaned her head against the Pumpkin King's bony shoulder and let herself dreamily live in the present. Her affection for Jack had been growing like the flowers in her cemetery garden: starting as shy seeds, flourishing with every look and kind word, and now bursting into bloom. She imagined a great future of never again being locked away in Dr. Finkelstein's castle, and being free to explore and dance and celebrate, just like all the townsfolk, with her and Jack always there for each other through the darkest of nights.

As they stood gazing at each other, Zero flew off into the sky, his pumpkin nose shining as brightly as the first star ever to look down on the land of nightmares.

That night, every resident of Halloween Town fell asleep to a soft melody being performed by the Undead Ensemble, which played a serenade for Jack and Sally and everyone who treasured the beautiful darkness of Halloween.

ABOUT THE AUTHOR

Megan Shepherd is a *New York Times* best-selling and Carnegie Medal–nominated author who grew up in her family's independent bookstore in the Blue Ridge Mountains. She is the author of many acclaimed novels and now lives and writes on a historic farm outside Asheville, North Carolina, with her family, an especially scruffy dog, and several ghosts. Visit her online at www.meganshepherd.com.